BOOK GiRL

and the Corrupted Angel

Mizuki Nomura

Konoha Inoue

If Tohko were here...

The snacks you've been putting in the mailbox this whole time have been really good.

The Book Girl, Tohko Amano

I ate them up and imagined that even though I'm not around, you're having fun... that something good must have happened to you.

Keiichi Mariya

"So the angel doesn't sing anymore. He mustn't."

"But I think Yuka might be with this angel."

Nanase Kotobuki

Shiro Omi

"She told me,
'My teacher is an
angel of music.'"

"You're going
to get hurt.
And not just
you. Nanase
Kotobuki
will, too."

Shoko Kagami

Did I want to know that?
No matter how intense the truth might be?
Even if I was beset by suffering and despair
even greater than I'd felt up till now, and it laid me
out to the point that I couldn't get back up?

But learning the truth
wasn't necessarily the right thing—

STUDYING FOR HER EXAMS

TOHKO...?

TOHKO AMANO

F

OYO, THIS PART'S DELICIOUS.

Contents

BOOK girL

and the Corrupted Angel

Mizuki Nomura

Illustrations by Miho Takeoka

Yen
Press
NEW YORK

Book Girl and the Corrupted Angel
Story: MIZUKI NOMURA
Illustration: MIHO TAKEOKA

Translation by Karen McGillicuddy

Bungakushoujo to kegarena no ange ©2007 Mizuki Nomura. All rights reserved.
First published in Japan in 2007 by ENTERBRAIN, INC., Tokyo.
English translation rights arranged with ENTERBRAIN, INC. through Tuttle-Mori Agency, Inc., Tokyo.

English translation © 2012 by Hachette Book Group, Inc.

Yen Press
Hachette Book Group
237 Park Avenue, New York, NY 10017

www.HachetteBookGroup.com
www.YenPress.com.

Yen Press is an imprint of Hachette Book Group, Inc. The Yen Press name and logo are trademarks of Hachette Book Group, Inc.

First Yen Press Edition: January 2012

Library of Congress Cataloging-in-Publication Data

Nomura, Mizuki.
  [Bungakushoujo to kegarena no ange. English]
  Book Girl and the corrupted angel / Mizuki Nomura ; illustrations, Miho Takeoka ; [translation by Karen McGillicuddy]. -- 1st Yen Press ed.
    p. cm.
  Summary: When Konoha takes a break from the literary club, whose president is a book-eating goblin, he becomes swept up in a mystery that unfolds as if from the pages of Gaston Leroux's classic novel, "The Phantom of the Opera."
  ISBN 978-0-316-07694-4
  [1. Mystery and detective stories. 2. Books and reading--Fiction. 3. Supernatural--Fiction. 4. Goblins--Fiction. 5. Japan--Fiction.] I. Takeoka, Miho, ill. II. McGillicuddy, Karen. III. Title.
  PZ7.N728Bnc 2012
  [Fic]--dc23   2011017188

10 9 8 7 6 5 4 3 2 1

RRD-C

Printed in the United States of America

and the Corrupted Angel

Mizuki Nomura

Illustrations by Miho Takeoka

I've built many doorways and set out traps so that no one will be able to reach this place. That's what the angel said. This is a castle of darkness for the angel and I alone. Only within this yielding gloom can I lament the misfortune that has rained down all around me, only here am I permitted to scorn and pity the ugliness, the filthiness of how I smile and pretend at being pure in the light of day.

And only here can I continue to be Nanase's best friend.

Prologue—Memories for an Introduction—I Used to Be with an Angel

He was a man who straddled heaven and earth; that's how the diva described him.

For me, Miu had that role.

Out of all my classmates, Miu was the only one who seemed to be surrounded in pure white light. Her voice was the only one that caressed my ears like refreshing music flowing down from heaven. Each time my heart squeezed tight at the words she spoke, I thought how special Miu was, how different from anyone else.

I knew she was an angel and that she was hiding invisible wings against her back.

How else could a girl my age create such beautiful stories so lightheartedly, so freely?

Having Miu beside me, having her look at me with her teasing, kittenish eyes; say my name in her sweet, clear voice; and twine her arm through mine like it was the most natural thing in the world—for me, it was a state of grace, a miracle granted by God, and I thought life would go on like that forever.

But how much did I know of the truth about Miu?

What kind of girl was the real Miu?

That serene summer afternoon in my third year of middle school, the peaceful routine Miu and I shared shattered in the worst possible way.

Miu jumped off the roof of our school, and I watched her go, helpless to act.

I retreated into my room after that, until at the end of winter, I somehow managed to drag myself from the pit my room had become with its curtains forever shut. I took my exams, I advanced to high school, and in so doing, I met Tohko Amano.

Called a book girl, loving every book in the world without exception, she was another girl who traveled freely between heaven and earth on the shining wings of imagination.

Chapter 1–Don't Ever Forget the Snack

"Oh—it's a sugar tart."

Tohko beamed happily after tearing off a corner of the lined paper.

"There's a rhythmical texture of rich red and black sugar and crushed walnuts inside a crumbly tart shell," she murmured with a sigh, tearing the paper up into precious strips and bringing them to her lips. "Each time I bite into it, there's a rustic sweetness that spreads over my tongue...Even though it's pretty sweet, there's a superb balance that keeps it from being overwhelming."

Rrrip. Flp-flp-flp. Gulp.

The otherworldly sounds resonated softly in the cramped room, which was practically buried under mounds of books.

Tohko is a goblin who eats stories.

She would argue, "I am *not* a goblin—I'm just an ordinary book girl!" but the way she munched ravenously on paper with writing on it looked nothing like a legitimate high school girl.

"Did you know that a sugar tart is called a *tarte sucrée*? *Sucre* means sugar in French. The surface is lightly burned to make it crisp, but that accent is amazing, too. Today is a success! Well done, Konoha!"

5

Apparently the "snack" I'd written on the three prompts "a campfire," "a reindeer," and "a speed-eating contest" had met with Tohko's approval.

After losing a speed-eating contest, a reindeer roams in solitude through a forest at night until he encounters his girlfriend who's been steadfastly waiting for him at a campfire.

After writing such a treacly story, I couldn't be happy with her praise.

Maybe it should have been more twisted...

Since I always made her whine, "Yuuuuck!" by adding in a weird ending, I did want to write the kind of sweet story Tohko liked occasionally, but...

"I've never heard of a *tarte sucrée*. It's just a coincidence that it tastes like that. I actually meant for the girl to hit him with a flaming piece of firewood and make him into reindeer soup. My time ran out right when I got to them meeting," I said brusquely, picking up my paper and putting my pencil away in its case.

Tohko was sitting on a fold-up chair at the window with her knees drawn up to her chest, eating her snack. But when I said that, she paled, a scrap of paper still in her mouth.

"But why would you want to pour wasabi-flavored ketchup all over this perfect sugar tart?"

Hunching her thin shoulders and shaking her long braids that hung past her hips, she acted petulant and terrified, but then her eyes suddenly crinkled like a cat basking in a sunbeam again.

"I'm glad it ended when the reindeer was happy. It was really, totally sweet and delicious."

When she looked at me like that, something tickled deep in my heart and I felt more uncomfortable than I could say.

Okay, next time I'm definitely gonna do a messy horror story.

"Yummm! That was sooo good!"

Unaware of my plans, Tohko gulped down the very last bite, her face a picture of joy.

"I'm glad." *But next time's gonna be a gory horror story, so...,* I murmured in my heart, putting on a bright smile. But just then—

"Now I can put the club on hiatus with a clear conscience," Tohko said offhandedly.

"What?"

"Well, I'm a third-year, right? I've got to focus on my exams soon."

"You haven't *started* focusing yet?!"

I gaped at her. It was December! There were only two months or so left before exams! But she'd been in the clubroom ripping up and munching on books as she expounded on them till all hours, so I'd thought she had gotten in on a recommendation somewhere. But no...

"You mean you're actually taking exams?!"

"Of course. I'm a dedicated student," she declared majestically, her face unflappable. Man, I'd had no idea she was this cavalier...

When she saw my shoulders slump, Tohko started talking like she was a mature young woman.

"Don't lose heart, Konoha. I completely understand how sad you must feel that you won't be able to see your beloved president. And I won't be able to eat your snacks—I mean, being away from this dear, familiar clubroom pains me deeply.

"But you know, a person can't just skip around through sweet books. Sometimes they have to read every word of Takuboku Ishikawa's *Sad Toys* or *A Handful of Sand*.

"Yes—it's like eating an endless salad of pickled radish and carrot slivers piled up on rice. As you taste the hardships of life in the ephemerality of the vinegar-soaked radish and the crispness of the carrots, the sweetness of the little pinch of sugar mixed in gives you courage, and you eat it taking one bite, and

7

then another. Salad is really good for you. You should try some, Konoha."

"I have no idea what you're talking about!"

"I'm talking about doing our best to eat a salad in the winter so we'll have a happy spring."

"Me eating salad isn't going to improve your test performance. Besides, didn't Takuboku Ishikawa die in poverty? You're not getting rewarded. You're gonna fail."

"Waaah! Don't say such awful things to a delicate student studying for exams!"

Tohko curled up into a ball, covering her ears with both hands.

"Oh, whatever…Just go home already and start studying," I said apathetically.

Suddenly her face became more grown-up and she chortled.

"Yes, thank you. I will."

She slipped her small feet, shod only in school socks, into the slippers she had kicked off and then stood up.

Then she held three pages of essay paper out to me.

"Huh? What's that?"

"It's a list of provisions. You want to do something to help your beloved president, don't you, Konoha?"

Crayon, fire station, limbo dance—essence of a piping hot fondant au chocolat.

Butterfly, Mount Fear, a surfer—essence of a fluffy, therapeutic vanilla soufflé.

Flashlight, rafflesia, English test—essence of a luxury fruit parfait.

The page was packed with words like that!

I thought she was going to advance spiritually by eating salad!

"Write one each day, okay? Gimme suuupersweet snacks. I'm really looking forward to it! Oh, and don't worry. I'm not retiring from the club until graduation."

She beamed and waved vigorously at me, then left the room; blankly, I watched the braided goblin go.

"What a selfish person!" I ranted at Akutagawa the next morning.

"Who?"

"Tohko! I never wanted to join any club at all. But then she dragged me into a creepy club like the book club and makes me write stories every day, and she expounds on books while she reads them, and now she's talking about putting the club on hiatus out of nowhere, and while it's out, I have to write stories 'cos she wants to read them or whatever."

"You upset?"

"You bet I am."

"But you're writing them?"

Akutagawa's eyes dropped to the notebook sitting open on my desk.

I subtly moved my hands to cover the improv story I'd started writing.

"Wh-what choice do I have? If I don't, she'll just throw a tantrum and say I lack respect for my president or that it was my fault she couldn't focus on her exams. She would."

Akutagawa's handsome face broke into a grin.

"You're usually so stoic, Inoue. But as soon as Tohko comes up, you start acting like a little kid."

"What's that supposed to mean? Tohko's the one who acts like a child. I'm babysitting her."

"Oh yeah?"

"Yeah!"

"Well, let's just say that's true. Anyway, did you get my text?"

"What?"

I quickly pulled my cell phone out of my uniform pocket.

It was a brand-new midnight-blue phone I'd just purchased a few days earlier. Until now I'd always said there was no reason for me to have one, but I had become friends with Akutagawa and started to realize it might be more convenient to have one, so my parents had gotten a family plan for me.

"Sorry, I'm not used to checking for messages. Yesterday I sent you that I picked an e-mail, right?"

When I checked my new messages, I saw there was a text from Akutagawa and also one from Maika, my little sister, for some reason. She was in elementary school, but in order to coordinate taking her to her swim classes and picking her up afterward, our parents had bought her a cell phone, too. She'd probably sent me a message because she was so happy to have it. So *that* was why she had scowled at me this morning over her toast slathered with tangerine jelly. Ack—I'd have to answer her later. If she started sulking over that, it would be a huge pain.

"Here's your message. Hey, you use smilies? I never would have thought that."

Akutagawa looked embarrassed.

"My sisters told me my messages were too formal, so I tried to do better. They're pretty useful."

"Oh yeah? Then I'll get my little sister to teach me some and find some crazy ones to send you."

"Looking forward to it."

Just then a clump of girls from our class came over.

"Hey, Inoue! You bought a cell phone! Oh wow, it's the latest model! Nice!"

"Will you give me your e-mail, Inoue?"

"Me, too! Please, Inoue?"

They surrounded me so suddenly that it baffled me.

Akutagawa was one thing, but why me? Girls had never been interested in me before.

10

"Give it to Nanase, too!"

Kotobuki was at the back of the group, but Mori dragged her forward. Kotobuki freaked out.

"Th-that's okay! Even if he tells me his e-mail, I'd never use it."

"Come on! Everyone's sharing e-mails, so you have to, too!"

"Yeah. You don't wanna get left out of the loop. Let me see your phone."

"I...I said no."

"Geez, you're so obnoxious. Aaand, found it!"

Mori had shoved her hand into Kotobuki's pocket and pulled out her cell phone.

"Hey, quit it! Give that back, Mori!"

Um...she didn't have to go *that* far. Kotobuki really seemed upset.

Just then...

"Nanaseee! Someone to see youuu!"

When she saw the kind-looking man standing in the hall dressed in a casual suit, Kotobuki made a disgusted face. Then she glared at me hurriedly, looked over at him and then back at me; then she turned back to him and then to me.

"They're calling you, Kotobuki."

"I...I don't need you to tell me that!" she snapped, then pressed her lips together and made a dash to the hallway.

"Oh! It's Marmar!"

"Whoa! What does he want with Nanase, I wonder?"

Mr. Keiichi Mariya had been teaching music since last spring. He had refined features and was popular with the girls. There were also rumors that he was a little eccentric, but...

"Marmar is definitely interested in Nanase!"

"Totally. He called her 'Nanase' once by accident, and he's

always looking at her during class. He's after her constantly, too. What are you gonna do about it, Inoue?"

"Huh? Wh…what am I—?"

"Nanase is suuuperpopular with boys. I mean, she's gorgeous, and the fact that she's always got her guard up just makes them want more. If you're not careful, things could get bad."

"Get bad how?"

"Argh, what are those two *talking* about? This is killing me."

Mori and the others were unusually worked up. It was all gibberish to me. Beside me, Akutagawa shrugged.

Mr. Mariya had his hands pressed together in front of him— he looked like he was asking Kotobuki for a favor. But Kotobuki barely seemed to be listening and was stealing glances in my direction. She was frowning, her lips pursed. I was just thinking how much she looked like my little sister, who had glanced up at me and sulked in disappointment that morning, when Mr. Mariya suddenly looked over at me.

A perplexed look came over his face, and then he waved me over with a hand, the wrist of which was encircled by an expensive-looking watch.

Me? I asked with a glance, and he nodded with a gentle, congenial smile.

Still confused, I went out to the hall and asked, "Do you need me?"

He answered in a sweet, lighthearted voice that tickled at my ears. "Would you be willing to give me a hand with something after school, Inoue? I'd like you to organize the papers in the music room."

"Hold on—why're you asking *Inoue*?" Kotobuki wailed, aghast.

"You've been making eye contact with Inoue for a while now, Nanase. And you said it was too much for one person to do alone and that you wanted help."

"I did not! And anyway, I never said I would do it."

"Oh? Then why do your eyes keep going back to Inoue?"

"I...I..."

"You don't mind helping, do you, Inoue?"

Drawn in by his cheerful voice and friendly smile, I surprised myself when I reflexively answered, "Uh, what? No."

Wait—did I just agree? Oh god! Kotobuki pursed her lips and glared at me.

"Great, thanks. It would be marvelous if you could start right away after school today. There's quite a bit to do, so I need you two to do your best."

Mr. Mariya clapped me on the back, looking pleased with himself.

"This is your fault, Inoue."

It was after school, and Kotobuki was extremely angry.

The music room in the southeast corner of the second floor was packed with tons of cardboard boxes. Our job was to sort the papers crammed in each box and put them into files.

"S-sorry...but he asked you to do it first..."

"If you hadn't agreed, I would have said no. Geez, as if I wanted to work with you!"

Prickling with rage, she opened a box and started piling the papers in it on the floor. Mr. Mariya talked in a vibrantly cheerful voice.

"This is great. I'm so glad you could help, Nanase. You do enjoy bluntness, don't you? It's so charming the way that you sulk."

"I've got no interest in old men! And stop calling me Nanase!"

"Oh, I'm sorry. I thought Nanase was your last name and somehow just remembered you that way."

"My full name was written on the class roll, though!"

"Hmm, was it?"

13

"Grrrr!"

Kotobuki growled in irritation, whirling to turn her back on him. He drew nearer to me and whispered in amusement, "She's adorable when she loses her temper, don't you think? It thrills me being rejected by a girl like that; it makes me want to squeeze her tight."

"Mr. Mariya... I'm not sure a teacher should be saying things like that."

"A teacher is nothing but an adult man once he leaves the classroom, Inoue."

"Then please don't say that until after you leave the building."

As we whispered to each other, our faces pressed close together, Kotobuki turned slooowly back around.

The very same instant, Mr. Mariya shouted gleefully, "Oh, what's this, Nanase? Are you curious what Inoue and I are talking about? We were just observing how cute you are. Isn't that right, Inoue?"

"Er, uh—that is—" I was trapped.

"N-no! I don't care."

Kotobuki quickly turned her back on us.

"Oh! Nanase, there's a worm on your thigh."

"Eek!"

Kotobuki jumped and shook out her skirt. Her eyes were positively brimming with tears.

"Hmmm, so you don't like worms then. I suspected as much. I'm good at guessing where a girl's tastes lie. In any case, it's commonly thought that worms hibernate in the winter and stop moving around, so you needn't worry."

"Grrrr. Y-you molester!"

She balled up a piece of paper and hurled it at him, but Mr. Mariya dodged it easily. The ball landed right in my face.

"Ow!"

Kotobuki looked frantic, her face bright red, and she turned

14

her back on me, muttering, "Ack—! Y-you're such a klutz, Inoue! Why didn't you dodge?"

Or so it seemed until she turned to glance back worriedly and then hurriedly turned around again.

"See? Isn't she cute?"

Mr. Mariya rested a hand on my shoulder and winked.

Kotobuki…he's toying with you, I thought.

I felt bad for her. But…Mr. Mariya was right: Kotobuki looked cute when she was angry or flustered. So that's the kind of girl Kotobuki is. I could see now why the boys in our class made so much noise about how great Nanase Kotobuki was…

"Let's take a break."

After we'd been working away for about an hour, Mr. Mariya poured some tea into paper cups for us.

I thought it might be tea with milk, but the color and aroma were both rich and it tasted sweet. There was the light fragrance of cinnamon. Oh, and maybe there was some ginger in there, too.

"This is called chai. It's a sweet, boiled tea with milk that's drunk in India. What do you think?"

"It's very good."

It seemed like something Tohko would like. Sweet, warm, relaxing, melting away fatigue…

Mr. Mariya's eyes crinkled as he smiled.

"I'm glad. I love serving my guests chai. Did it meet with your approval also, Nanase?"

"…It's good."

"If you married me, you'd be able to drink it every day."

"Never! That will never, ever happen!"

Kotobuki howled like a cat with its fur standing on end, but Mr. Mariya was undaunted.

"Oh yes. A friend of mine sent me some tickets to the opera.

It's a student recital, but the lead tenor is a professional making a guest appearance. Would you like to go, Nanase?"

He held the tickets up between his fingers, and Kotobuki shot a sideways glance at them, maybe a little bit interested.

"...I have some, too."

Mr. Mariya made a surprised face.

"Oh? What a coincidence. Do you like the opera? We have something in common then. Perhaps it's fate."

Kotobuki quickly denied it.

"No, I—one of my friends is performing, so I bought my own ticket!"

"Oh my, one of your friends is a student at the Shirafuji Music Academy high school? I'm an alumnus there! Incidentally, is she pretty?"

"So what if she is?!"

"Oh, I just thought it would be nice for the three of us to go get Nepalese food together. Your friend is available, isn't she?"

"Yuka has a boyfriend! Even if she didn't, I would never introduce a lazy music teacher who puts in earplugs in order to take naps during music classes to my best friend!"

"I'm a student of Buddhism, so when I hear Christian hymns, a beanstalk grows out of my belly."

"I've never heard of that before!"

"That's because it's not true."

"Grrrr!"

"M-Mr. Mariya, maybe you should stop. Don't start waving your fists around, either, Kotobuki. Okay?"

Sensing the unquiet in the air, I quickly stepped into the fray. Kotobuki suddenly flushed and lowered her hands to sweep off her skirt; then she returned to the work with obvious haste.

Through a cloud of sweet-smelling steam, Mr. Mariya smiled serenely as he watched Kotobuki's reaction.

"Marmar studied vocals. He studied abroad in Paris while he was in college, and he even won a competition while he was over there!"

At lunch the next day, while I ate my packed lunch with Akutagawa, Mori and her friends came purposefully over to us and started talking about Mr. Mariya.

"His parents are musicians, too, and I've heard that people called him a genius. Apparently he sings in a supersweet, liquid tenor. Marmar could have been as big as a pop star when he made his professional debut. Why did he become a teacher, you think? What a total waste!"

"Oh, but really, for a boyfriend you want a totally normal guy, not an older heartthrob with a past. Don't give up, Inoue!"

"Yeah. Nanase doesn't go for brand-name stuff, so relax and go for it."

"Oh! Nanase's back! Say hi to her for us, Inoue."

Gaping, I watched Mori and the others patter off.

"Akutagawa, what just happened...?"

"Pretty sure I followed, but I can't say. Kotobuki would never forgive me."

Akutagawa set down his chopsticks, looking sorry.

But...oh, I thought sluggishly, still holding my lettuce and scrambled egg sandwich. *Mr. Mariya had also been called a genius.*

Classes were over for the day. After I dropped off the improv story for Tohko's provisions in the relationship advice box that had been set up without permission in the school yard, I went to the music room, where a boy I didn't recognize stood in front of the door.

He was about my height. He had bright, colorless hair, was thin, and wore glasses—a perfectly ordinary student with no distinguishing features.

He kept his face down and glided past me like a breeze.

Huh? Didn't that guy have some reason for being at the music room...?

When I opened the door, I saw Mr. Mariya sitting on a fold-up chair, drinking chai. He had a finger pressed to his lip, as if he was thinking about something, and the sight of him spacing out unguardedly called to mind a certain braided book girl, and I smirked. A heavy-looking watch glinted at his wrist.

"Hmm? By yourself, Inoue? Where's Nanase?"

"She said she had to take care of something and was going to be late."

"Ah, good. I thought I might have tormented her a little too much yesterday, and she'd run away on me. It was a chilling thought."

"If you realize what you're doing, why don't you take some responsibility?"

"Oh, but her reactions are so much fun I can't help myself."

He grinned at me, his eyes seeming to declare, "It's a secret."

Ever since the day before, Mr. Mariya had been giving me that same sort of familiar look, as if he was a kindly older brother. Whenever he did, it made my chest squirm a little.

"I heard that you won a competition abroad, and people used to call you a genius."

"Ha-ha, it's been said, yes."

Mister Mariya laughed lightly.

His smile was so natural I couldn't stop myself from asking, "Why didn't you go professional?"

The moment it was said, a thorn shot through my heart. As I waited for his answer, I held my breath completely in earnest.

Because I had once been called a genius, too.

It was in the spring of my third year that I, an ordinary middle schooler, had been swallowed up by a gigantic wave.

At fourteen years old, I won the new author's prize of a literary magazine that I'd entered on a whim, their youngest winner ever, and because my pen name was Miu Inoue—a girl's name—I was crowned with the exaggerated title of a mysterious genius in the body of a masked, young female author, and I became famous throughout the country.

Now that more than two years had gone by, I was spending my days peaceably again. I'd even made friends and learned how to laugh.

How had it been for Mr. Mariya?

He'd been hailed as a genius by everyone around him and had great things expected of his future, so why had he become a teacher?

What did he think about it all now?

Through the sweet-smelling steam, Mr. Mariya's lips bent into a soft smile.

"I wanted the time I spent at leisure with the person I loved to be more important than anything. Florid strangers, gut-wrenching practices, intense schedules—they weren't for me."

His voice was clear and unwavering.

His eyes narrowed in a gentle smile like gooey, golden honey, and he raised his paper cup as if in a toast.

"So I can affirm that I have no regrets about my decision. So long as I have a cup of chai, life is wonderful, and an ordinary life beats anything else."

His words and his voice penetrated my heart like beams of light, and like the sweet chai that gave off the aroma of cinnamon, they seeped slowly and warmly into every corner of my body, leaving a sharp excitement behind.

I couldn't take my eyes from Mr. Mariya's smile.

Man, that would be great.

Someday, I wanted to be able to validate my own life like he had.

I wanted to spend every day in easy normalcy while cherishing the gentleness of the ordinary.

Mr. Mariya, who I'd only thought of as a weirdo, seemed like a very broad-minded, generous person.

Finally Kotobuki appeared, out of breath.

"Hello, Nanase. You were so eager to see me that you rushed that much to get here?"

"N-no, I—"

"Oh no, is that a worm?"

"Eek!"

"Kotobuki, worms are hibernating right now."

"Er...shut up, Inoue!"

Mr. Mariya was teasing Kotobuki the same as he had yesterday.

Kotobuki was getting red faced and angry. I was getting into the middle of things...

This kind of trivial interaction was fun, warm, and comfortable.

Hello, Konoha.

Thank you for the snacks in the mailbox.

For the essence of fresh mint jelly in "school gate," "whale," and "bungee jumping."

The jelly was sweet, and it was more like a thick milk tea than mint, but it melted away on my tongue and tasted like cinnamon and ginger and tasted *great*. It was just like chai. The last words were jelly made gooey by the heat, dropping warmly into my belly. I felt so happy. Thank you.

I got an F on my prep class practice test, so I was a little depressed. Eating your story cheered me up, though. Write me another good one.

Tohko

Whoa! She saw right through me.

After school, I read the letter from Tohko that was in the mailbox, and my cheeks grew slowly warmer. It tasted like chai... Well, of course it did, though I hadn't been aware of it.

And then she got an F. *Are you going to be all right, Tohko?*

If you upset your stomach before an exam, you'll be in a real jam, so you should lay off the special platters of ghosts for a while.

I dropped off the new snack I'd put together during class and headed to the music room.

The angel brought me a fir tree.

Last night I was so depressed about my job, he probably wanted to cheer me up. My angel knows everything about me. And I can tell my angel anything.

Things I can't even tell Nanase—ugly things, dirty things, everything.

It's still early for Christmas, but the angel and I dug a hole in the ground and planted the fir tree. Our precious Christmas tree.

Tomorrow I promised I would decorate it with angel wings, crystal churches, gold bells, and stars, and then we would have to put up lights.

The angel doesn't believe in God, so he says that he hates Christmas and hymns. Whenever I sing them, he covers his ears and screams for me to stop. I can't believe in God, either, but I like Christmas. I could stare at the lights on the tree all

night long. When I do, it feels very pure and holy, even though I don't believe in God. It's like my spirit is being sucked up into the light.

I wish I could have lived in the tree. If I had, I'm positive my ugliness would melt away into the white light.

I'm spending Christmas Eve this year with my boyfriend.
I'm spending Christmas with Nanase.

I wonder if things are going well with Nanase and Inoue? Although yesterday on the phone, she was depressed because she said, "I glared at him *again*" and "I said something mean *again*."

Nanase is supercute and nice, so if she was just a little more proactive, I'm sure Inoue would fall for her.

When I told her I thought it would be nice to be able to go on a double date—her and Inoue and me and my boyfriend—I felt like an awful person for lying. My heart hurt, and I felt like crying. I didn't know what to do.

⇒◆⇐

"You're really close with Mr. Mariya, huh, Kotobuki?"

"Wh-what?! How can you say that?! Of course, I'm not."

One hour later I was working with Kotobuki in the music room, which was warmed by the light of the sun.

Mr. Mariya had something to do in the teachers' office and had left, so Kotobuki and I were all alone in the room. Kotobuki was next to me, rummaging through papers, and she growled, "You sure there's nothing wrong with your eyes, Inoue?"

"Maybe. When you're with him, you seem more talkative than usual."

"W-well…"

She started to say something else, then turned sharply away with an "Am not" and fell silent.

She continued her work with tremendous energy in silence.

And now I remembered that there was something I wanted to ask her. How could I do it? I just had to commit and ask right now, I guess.

"Hey, Kotobuki."

"Wh-what?!"

"Where was it that you and I met in middle school? I've been thinking about it, but I can't remember."

Well, I'd said it.

But I wanted to take this opportunity to clear things up— the things Kotobuki had rambled tearfully about at our play rehearsal for the culture fair—

"I'm sure you don't remember, but it meant a lot to me."

"The girl who was always with you was the author Miu Inoue, wasn't she?!"

Why had Kotobuki mistaken Miu for Miu Inoue?

Why didn't I remember meeting Kotobuki?

Maybe the reason for her unnatural stubbornness lay there…

Her head hanging down, Kotobuki was as still as a stone. She bit down on her lip and paled.

Maybe I shouldn't have asked…

Just as I was beginning to regret it, she forced out a pained response.

"…the school emblem."

"Huh?"

"School emblem…still doesn't help you remember?"

"Um, you mean the school emblem that's a patch you stick on your uniform, right?"

Kotobuki's shoulders twitched.

"Hold on, I'm remembering right now. The emblem... hmm...hmmm..."

My middle school's emblem was in the shape of a maple. The color changed depending on the class year, and Kotobuki had met me in the...winter of my second year? In that case, the emblem was blue, so...

"God, just forget it."

Her agitated voice interrupted my thoughts.

Kotobuki's hands were balled up fiercely, and she was shaking.

"Y-you don't need to force yourself to remember," she said.

The air was frigid. I was bewildered.

Just then, Mr. Mariya returned.

"Sorry about that. I swiped a salty rice cake from the teachers' office, so let's have some tea. Oh—Nanase, what's the matter?"

Mr. Mariya's face closed in on hers to the point he was almost kissing her, and Kotobuki jerked away in a panic.

"I—it's nothing!"

"Oh, were you sad that I wasn't here?"

He laughed brightly, but she wailed, red faced, "I hate you! You pervert! No!"

She seemed slightly better, but Kotobuki didn't meet my gaze after that.

When the school building was tinted an angry red by the sun, the three of us left the music room together.

"Tomorrow and the day after, I'll be out on business, so we'll see each other next on Thursday. I know you can handle things."

"Okay. Bye, Mr. Mariya. Bye, Kotobuki."

"...Bye."

I parted ways with Mr. Mariya, who was going back to the teachers' office, and Kotobuki, who was heading back to the library. I was just starting to walk when I thought I felt someone watching me.

A gloomy, piercing face looked in my direction, but there was no one there.

Where was it coming from?

Standing in front of the stairs, I scanned the area when overhead I heard someone clucking his tongue and whispering low, as though the moaning of the wind.

"...What a heartwarming scene."

A shudder ran down my spine, and my skin prickled.

I turned my gaze upward and searched the stairs that circled up to the fourth floor, holding my breath, scouring them with my eyes. But there was no one there.

What...was that voice just now?

Who was it talking to? Me? Mr. Mariya? Or maybe Kotobuki?

I listened closely, but I couldn't even hear footsteps anymore.

———◆———

I got a call from my teacher about my customers. He's worried about me for a lot of reasons.

He is such a kind, wonderful person.

It's been so long since we've been on a date; he was kind of in a bad mood. Even if I touched his hand, he wouldn't loosen his fingers from around mine. He told me moodily to quit my job.

To cheer myself up, I decorated the entrance to the castle with lots of pictures.

Pictures of Nanase and me. Pictures of my angel and me. In every picture I was smiling happily, and whenever I looked at

26

them, I could think, *Wow, the girl in these pictures is so happy,* and I became happy.

But the pictures with him were the only ones that made me feel like my heart was ripping in half, and I couldn't put them up.

Instead, I put up photos of blue roses.

It was a lie of a color, a white rose that someone had dyed blue, but it was pretty.

Years ago, a *blue rose* was used to mean *something unusual* or *something impossible,* but now that people have succeeded in making blue roses by altering the genes, I heard that the flower's meaning had changed as well to mean *miracle* or *God's blessing.*

But in the pictures I'd seen of the flowers on the Internet, the rose was purplish and didn't look like an innocent blue at all...

So, maybe a blue rose still means *something unusual* after all.

To myself, I whispered the line that Christine says to Raoul.

"Our love is too tragic for this world. Let us away into the sky...Perhaps there even our love may be easily realized!"

I only hope that Nanase's love goes well.

⊰•◦•⊱

How could I make up with Kotobuki?

After class the next day, I walked down the hall stewing.

Kotobuki still seemed to be bothered by what happened yesterday, and she'd avoided me even in class.

Mori had come over to worriedly ask if Kotobuki and I had had a fight, but I couldn't really answer. Mori seemed frustrated, too, and she said, "Well, Nanase shuts down when she gets stressed out. I dunno what happened, but don't take it personally, okay?"

Suddenly I felt something poking into the back of my neck and I jumped up.

"Argh!"

I turned and saw a petite girl with fluffy hair hugging a dandelion-colored binder to her chest and grinning up at me. It was Takeda, the first-year.

"Hellooo, Konoha. Heh-heh-heh...I heard about Nanase."

"Takeda!...Wh-what do you mean? What did you hear?"

"I heard you're going on dates behind closed doors with Nanase in the music room. Not bad! Or did you choke up already?"

She prodded me in the ribs with her elbow.

"Cut it out, Takeda. Everybody's staring. They're not dates. We're just helping Mr. Mariya, the music teacher. He's always there, and anyway what do you mean 'choke up'?"

Just then, the cell phone in my shirt pocket rang with an incoming message.

I apologized, then checked the new message. My heart skipped. *What the—? A text from Kotobuki?!*

I hurried to read it.

This is Nanase.
I think it looked like I was ignoring you today. Sorry.
(-_-);;
Actually, I...(>_<)
Could you come to the library today? (^_-)
There's something I really need to talk to you about.
(*^_^*)

Wh-what was this?!

As I descended into panic, the smiles dancing and flashing in my brain, Takeda pointed a finger at me and said, "Ah! You're choking."

What was going on with Kotobuki?

Even though she'd started talking to me, I cut Takeda off and went to the library in a state of agitation. Kotobuki was working at the counter.

"I...Inoue—"

She looked horribly surprised, her eyes widening in panic. When I saw her face, I was so rattled it was as if my heart had taken over my entire body, and blood rushed into my head with frightening speed.

"Wh-what is it? You returning a book?" she asked.

"Well...I got your text about how there was something you wanted to talk about."

"Huh? From who?"

"What? From you. You asked if I could come to the library."

"What?!" she shrieked suddenly. She immediately clapped both hands over her mouth and said in a whisper, "I...didn't send any texts like that."

"But it came from your e-mail address a few minutes ago..."

I was confused, too. What was going on?

"No way. You must be wrong. Why would I send you—"

Kotobuki got indignant and glowered at me, when suddenly Mori and the others flocked over to the counter.

"Oh! Inoue's here! What *luck*!"

"Hey, great, Nanase! Wasn't there something important you wanted to tell him?"

"Let us handle the desk, and you can go talk over there. Go on!"

Kotobuki's eyes turned suddenly sharp.

"Mori, were you the one who sent Inoue a text on my phone?"

The frigid tone of her voice put Mori at a loss for words.

29

"Uh, well…"

"A couple minutes ago, you said you forgot your phone and asked to borrow mine."

"I—I'm sorry! You haven't been able to talk to Inoue, so…"

Kotobuki's cheeks flared, and her fierce cry cut through the air.

"Don't do stupid stuff like that! I *hate* Inoue!"

The words stabbed into my ears, and my brain felt like it was burning.

Everyone around the counter fell silent, and Kotobuki looked at me with blank eyes. Then her face suddenly crumbled. Looking as if she was about to burst into tears, she bit down firmly on her lower lip, then rushed from the counter and ran out of the library without another word.

"Nanase! Wait!"

Mori and the others hurried after her. I wondered what to do, whether I should go, too. But—

Just then, I heard a low voice beside me.

"You're…awful."

I turned to look over in surprise and saw a boy wearing glasses, glaring at me with cold, piercing eyes.

I gasped.

Wasn't he the student I'd seen outside the music room?

And that voice! It was like the voice I'd heard yesterday at the stairs!

I stiffened. He kept his eyes fixed irritably on me, gave a disgusted scoff, and went behind the counter. Then he turned his cold face down and began the work of a library aide.

I still didn't understand how I had attracted his animosity, and I watched him with a chill.

A last-minute job came up.

When I meet a new customer, I'm always a little afraid. Because they might grab my hair and punch me until my face swells up and leave me barefoot in a pitch-dark field.

Because the three-faced guy might smile unpleasantly and say, "Paying three times the fee ought to cover it."

I wondered if this was what it felt like to have your skin flayed off and your limbs shredded and eaten while you're still alive. If I screamed, my throat would be crushed. So I gritted my teeth, pressed my lips together, and simply cried, but far from losing interest, I was beaten even harder. To them, I was a nameless, inhuman pig. No, I knew other people thought the same...

I had a text and voice mail from Nanase. She was in total disarray about Inoue and it sounded like she was going to cry any second. Apparently her friends from class had said something. She said she wanted to see me.

I want to fly to her side right this second and listen to her troubles until dawn if I have to. I want to stroke her hair and comfort her.

I can't stand it when Nanase cries. I feel a physical pain, and it knocks the breath out of me.

But it's impossible right now. If I don't go out, I'll be late.

I texted Nanase that I would call her later.

I have to send him a text, too.

I'm not good for him. Whenever I'm with him, the filth that clings to my body corrupts his purity and nobility. Each time his clean fingers gently touch me, despair wells up in me that I'm unworthy of being loved and I want to die.

I don't want to sully his name. I don't want to demean him. I can't do that! Ever!

I care for him more than I can say. I believe that for his sake I could go on bearing things even more painful than death, and so some day, I'll have to leave him.

My love is too tragic for this world. Unless I can away into the sky, I'll never be clean.

But I'm sorry. Let me stay with you a little longer—just a little bit longer. Let me touch your hand. Just until the recital is over.

I really won't be in time now.

I'll see you later, Nanase.

Chapter 2–The Diva's Whereabouts

The next morning, I left home earlier than usual.

Even after I'd gotten home yesterday, the only thing on my mind had been the image of Kotobuki's face as she was on the verge of breaking into tears. It had stumped me. It had been a shock that Kotobuki seemed to be hurt worst—even more than me—and she'd said that she hated me in front of all those people. I almost felt like I'd forced her to say that...Even when I sat down at my desk to write Tohko's snack, I brooded over it, and my pencil didn't budge. The "butterfly," "Mount Fear," and "surfer" prompts—essence of fluffy, therapeutic vanilla soufflé that I had crafted through my grumbling—were a long way from fluffy, therapeuticness.

There was still time before class started. I would rewrite the story in the clubroom.

I felt the piercing cold of the air on my skin as I passed through the school's front gate, where I spotted Kotobuki.

Huh?

Below the thick, bleak clouds, Kotobuki was moving toward the front stairs on unsteady, wobbly legs. There was something strange about the way she acted.

My heart thrummed, and my steps grew naturally quicker as I went after her.

Kotobuki stood in front of the shoe lockers, her eyes empty.

In profile her face was pale and drained of energy.

"Kotobuki."

When I said her name, she started and looked up. "... Inoue."

Her voice was a hoarse murmur, and tears started welling up in her strong-willed eyes.

That caught me off guard.

"Wh...what's wrong? If you're upset about what happened yesterday..."

"...I'm not. It's Yuka..."

Yuka?

The next instant, Kotobuki had covered her face with both hands and burst out sobbing.

"Yuka's disappeared! I don't know what to do—I—I—"

"C'mon, what's wrong? What happened? Don't cry, okay? Can you tell me about it?"

I soothed Kotobuki as I held her hand and led her into the book club's room, then made her sit on a fold-up chair. She was bawling like a child.

Kotobuki curled up into a little quivering ball and soaked the sleeves of her coat and her uniform skirt with tears. She sobbed again and again until at last she told me what had happened.

That a friend of hers who went to a different school, Yuka Mito, had disappeared.

She said that after running out of the library yesterday, she'd gone to the Mitos' house.

But when she got there, a window was broken and the house was empty and there was no sign that anyone lived there anymore. Spooked, she asked a passing neighbor about it and was told that the Mitos had been unable to pay back a loan and had fled in the night two months ago.

"...*Hic*. I'd been texting Yuka every day, and I called her, and we even went shopping together last month. She never said a word about moving. *Hic*...I can't believe something like that would happen to Yuka's family...I tried to call her a bunch of times last night, but it went to voice mail every time. She didn't answer my text messages, either. Usually she answers right away! Where did she go?"

Kotobuki was an utter shambles. Her face was a mess, and she sobbed through her sniffling. She looked small and frail, as if she would shatter if someone didn't help her. Tears fell on her kneecaps peeking out from underneath her skirt.

The bell had already rung, and it was no longer even home-room—we were in the middle of first period now.

Before, I never would have imagined that *I* would be skipping class to be alone with a girl.

But I could hardly abandon Kotobuki when she was choking back her tears, without the faintest idea of what to do after the shock of her best friend's disappearance.

Maybe I felt it more deeply because of how she'd looked yesterday in the library.

"Don't cry, Kotobuki. We'll look for Mito together. Why don't we go to her school and ask people about her? I'll help you, okay?"

Kotobuki nodded imperceptibly and continued crying.

After getting home, I turned on my computer and did a search.

The high school Mito attended was a famous school that produced a great many professional musicians and was attached to the Shirafuji Music Academy. The classes were also structured around a focus on music, and there were a lot of students who studied abroad. The building featured on the school's home page had a luxurious Western-style exterior; I'd seen it used in TV shows before.

Mito had hoped to be a professional opera singer. An opera concert by the students was coming up at the school's auditorium, and she had gotten the lead role. She'd been busy with rehearsals and her part-time job lately, so apparently she hardly picked up the phone and often talked through text messages.

I clicked idly on the tab for enrollment and class fees, and my eyes bugged out. It was almost three times the amount as for a public school. It was double even compared to most private school fees! There were four people in the Mito family, and her father was an ordinary office worker. Apparently Mito had started her part-time job to earn money for school.

"Studying music sure is expensive."

I remembered the spacious music hall at Seijoh Academy. It was pretty amazing since a building that extravagant had been built with the donations of orchestra alumni. It was beyond what most people could ever conceive of in their daily lives, even though the orchestra had a strong connection to the Himekura family that ran the school.

As I deepened the search, my cell phone chimed with an incoming call.

The person I'd been waiting for was calling. When I put the phone to my ear, a bright voice flared out.

"Long time no see, Konoha. I'm shocked that *you* were the one who called *me*."

Ryuto Sakurai was the son of the family Tohko boarded with. This past summer, we had gotten to know each other after Tohko assaulted him with her schoolbag when he was starting trouble among some girls.

Ryuto sounded like he was grinning on the other end of the phone.

"Tohko said she didn't get a snack. She was PO'd. 'I was lookin' forward to it, too! Konoha's just awful! Awful! He's got no respect for his elders!' Her words."

Ryuto was mimicking Tohko's voice.

Great! I'd totally forgotten about the snack! I'd meant to rewrite the draft and drop it off in the mailbox, but it was still in my bag.

"I've been a little caught up with stuff, so I haven't had time."

"Oh, when she hears *that*, Tohko's gonna pout till her face pops. She'll say, 'But Konoha's snacks are my only pillar to face studying for exams! There's no joy left in my life now. My exams will be a failure. It's Konoha's faaaault!'"

"You're just making that up."

"Ohhh no, that's the cry of Tohko's heart. I mean, you are her author, Konoha," Ryuto said impudently.

Tohko's author.

My cheeks flushed at the words, though he'd said that to me before. What I wrote was just scribbling, and if I was going to be anything in the future, it wasn't an author.

Swallowing my bitter thoughts, I told Ryuto about everything that had happened.

"So, if you know anyone at the Shirafuji Music Academy high school, could you introduce me to them?"

"I'm shocked. You don't usually go to all that trouble."

"I...guess."

"'Cos I thought you were the type of guy who didn't wanna get involved with people."

My cheeks burned again. Up till now I'd been undeniably

hands-off. Something had definitely changed, just a little, after the culture fair when I'd become friends with Akutagawa.

Ryuto's voice was probing. "Might you by any chance have an *interest* in this Kotobuki girl?"

I quickly replied, "It's not like that. I just can't abandon her to this situation, so my opinion of Kotobuki doesn't really..."

"Hey, forget it. You want a favor. I'll help. I've got a contact at Shirafuji, so I'll try to get in touch."

I knew he would. He three- and four-timed so nonchalantly, and his entire year was just a slaughter.

The number of girls Ryuto had pull with and his ability to mobilize them had surprised me before. If he didn't know anybody, he made a sneak attack to chat them up and become friends. He was a person who did that sort of thing indifferently. Was he really younger than me?

"Thanks. I knew I could rely on you, Ryuto."

Ryuto let my automatic praise wash over him.

"However, I do have one condition."

He sounded a lot like Maki.

"What's that? I can help you with your homework if that's what you want."

"Nah, I've got tons of girls who do that for me already. Nothing like that. Konoha, do you have any plans for Christmas Eve?"

I was thrown off by his unexpected question.

"Christmas Eve? No..."

"Awesome! Can you keep it that way, then?"

"Please don't ask me to go to D—land with a boy on Christmas Eve and hold hands and watch the Electrical Parade."

"Ha-ha, that'd be great. Anyhow, just keep Christmas Eve open. Even if a girl with a way better chest than Tohko asks you out, you gotta shut her down."

"So you mean any girl over ten years old?"

"Oh, wow, harsh, Konoha. Tohko's super-self-conscious about that, and she does these exercises to make her breasts grow every day, so don't tease her about it, please."

"What kind of exercises…make her breasts grow?"

"Like, she puts her hands together in front of her chest then goes right, left, reeeal slooow. When I peek into her room, I see her doin' 'em with a real serious look on her face."

Picturing it made me feel dizzy. Could it be yoga?

"Anyhow, I'll text you once I get hold of my contact for that Shirafuji thing. So can you remember Tohko's snack? She's seriously lookin' forward to it. This is her little brother askin'," he finished in a joking tone, then hung up. It was fifty minutes later when I got a message from him—just as I had finished up the improv story for Tohko's snack.

Tomorrow at 4, wait at the main gate to the Shirafuji high school. A crazy good-looking girl's gonna come meet ya.

And so the next day after school, Kotobuki and I waited with a touch of nerves in front of the impressive stone gate for Ryuto's friend to appear.

Ever since the beginning of December, the sun had been going down earlier and earlier, so the school building was painted in the burgundy light of the setting sun. A sharp north wind was blowing, making Kotobuki's shoulders tremble.

"Are you cold?" I asked.

"I…I'm fine!" she answered awkwardly, shifting her gaze all over the place. I guess she was embarrassed about sobbing in front of me yesterday. She hadn't gotten a text from Mito today, either, so that made three days' interruption. That must have been making her frantic, too.

It was already ten minutes past the time we were supposed to meet this person. Any number of girls passed by us wearing coats over uniforms styled like ladylike dresses, but no one who looked right appeared. Ryuto had said she'd be "crazy good-looking" in his message, but I was starting to regret not asking her name when—

"Are you Inoue?"

Out of nowhere, a sensuous voice tickled down my spine, and I spun around.

"Looks like that's a yes. Sorry I'm late. I'm Ryu's friend, Shoko Kagami."

Her bright red lips lifted into a smile—a beautiful woman dressed in a close-fitting blouse, pants, and a long coat.

"Mind if I smoke?" she asked as soon as we'd gone into a nearby café and settled on a sofa.

"Uh…"

I looked over at Kotobuki, and she nodded.

"Go ahead."

Shoko's eyes crinkled indulgently when she saw that exchange.

"Thanks. I know they're bad for your throat, but I can't quit."

She put a slim, light-brand cigarette in her mouth and lit it with a silver lighter. Her movements were practiced, like a model's. She was absolutely an amazing beauty. Where had Ryuto met her?

Shoko was a voice teacher, and she knew Mito. She told us, frowning, how Mito had been out of school for a long time.

"It'll be ten days soon. Apparently she hasn't been back to the dorms, either. I've been worried about her, too."

"Yuka's staying in the dorms?" Kotobuki asked, her jaw tightening.

"Yes. Her parents moved this fall."

She told us with pain evident in her voice about how Mito's father had cosigned a loan for a friend, how the collectors had even barged into his office so he could no longer work.

The whole time, Kotobuki's face was pale, and her eyes were wide.

"Mito is supposed to be playing the lead in *Turandot* in this month's recital. She seems to have gotten a good teacher somehow, and her voice has changed dramatically since the summer. Until then, her singing was awful, as if it were crushing her throat, and she was stagnating. I was interested to know what studio her instructor was with or if it was a professional singer. When I asked her about singing though, Mito dodged the question and wouldn't tell me. She told me, 'My teacher is an angel of music.' I thought she was joking."

Kotobuki's shoulders jerked. Fear came into her eyes, as if she'd heard something baleful.

"What's wrong, Kotobuki?"

"It...it's nothing."

She forced out her reply in a pained voice, gripping the hem of her skirt tightly. It didn't look like it was nothing...

"She'd been cast as the lead, so she really had everything ahead of her. She even had the power to be a pro."

Shoko stubbed out the cigarette in disgust.

"I'm sorry. I need to get back. Let me see your phone, Inoue."

"Oh, sure."

I held it out to her, and she pressed the buttons like someone who'd had long practice; then she passed it back to me.

"I put in my number and e-mail address. If you find out anything about Mito, please get in touch. I'll do the same."

"Thank you. Um, I'd also like to talk to Mito's classmates if that's possible."

"All right. Can you come back to this café tomorrow?"

She picked up the check and stood. Then as if she'd suddenly

41

remembered something, she said, "Oh, you're at Seijoh, aren't you, Inoue? How's Marmar doing?"

"Do you know Mr. Mariya?"

Shoko's face broke into a smile.

"He was my underclassman in college. He was our rising star. Him and his pure, lighthearted tenor. They said he could be a symbol of Japanese opera."

"Mr. Mariya's doing good. He seems to be enjoying himself. He was just telling me, 'So long as I have a cup of chai, life is wonderful.'"

"Same as ever, then. While he was studying abroad in Paris, he went away somewhere out of the blue, then came back a year later with a blasé grin on his face. His hair was shaggy, and he'd been tanned dark brown. He laughed and said he'd traveled all over, but he was back now and whatever. It caused quite a stir."

Her face was kind and placid as she spoke.

"I wish Mito would come back with a smile just like he did," Shoko murmured, and then she left the café.

Outside, a north wind blew.

Goods decorated with red and gold ribbons and white cotton were displayed in the windows along the road. It would be Christmas soon.

"Kotobuki, do you know what she meant by 'angel of music'?" I asked, holding my scarf down securely with one hand so the wind blowing into our faces wouldn't send it flying.

After showing some signs of hesitation, Kotobuki, who walked bent forward for the same reason, stuttered out an answer. "...I think she means *Phantom of the Opera*."

"You mean the musical?"

I recalled the image of a man in black clothes wearing a white mask to hide his face, which I'd seen on TV commercials.

Kotobuki nodded yes with some difficulty.

"Yuka was a fan of the musical, and she'd read the play tons of times. She's even lent it to me before. In the story, there's an 'Angel of Music' who gives lessons to the heroine, who's a singer. Yuka always said how she wished she could have an Angel of Music of her own."

Kotobuki buried the lower half of her face in her scarf and shivered.

"And then…"

The way she spoke with her voice hushed, it seemed like she was afraid of the Angel of Music.

"During summer break this year, I got a weird e-mail from her. It said, 'Nanase, I've met my Angel of Music.'"

The sharp wind streamed past our ears. The frigid sound of the wind was like the distant howling of a beast, and it tore up Kotobuki's words.

"After that, whenever she talked about the angel, she was always really high-strung and would say stuff like 'My angel makes me sing like an instrument' or 'My angel will lead me to heaven'…It was like she was drunk. It wasn't normal."

"Did she tell you the person's name?"

Kotobuki shook her head. "No."

She pressed her lips together, and a sudden rage flared in her eyes. Then she said harshly, "But I think Yuka might be with this angel."

My angel makes me sing like the best masterpiece instruments.

Ever since that night we first met, it's always been that way.

Until that day, I'd thought of myself as a broken instrument.

43

As a piece of junk that would only wheeze, even if you blew into it with all you had.

But now it's different.

A coloratura like a clear, tumbling bead, a shining bel canto that stretches high and wide as far as it can go. A joyous voice. A rising voice. A twinkling voice. A voice like the wind, like light.

I sang every song imaginable with total ease and melted away to become one with the sky.

My angel unleashed the songs that had been shut away inside me, huddled there.

The more I sang, the clearer my heart and soul became; the more my head ached, the lighter my body grew. I was able to forget everything.

I am ecstatic, as if standing in the center of the stage illuminated by a pure white light, singing an aria. I am happy, and even so—it's terrifying.

If all of this is a dream and I was to wake up and it all faded like mist, I couldn't go on living.

⟫⋅⟪

Why had Mito chosen to stay behind here all alone, away from her family?

Did she want to continue singing that much?

But then, why had she disappeared after being chosen to play the lead in the recital?

As I lay in bed thinking these things over after I got home, I began reading the copy of *Phantom of the Opera* that I'd picked up at a bookstore on the way home.

The book was thick and stuffed with fine print. It looked like it would take some work to read it in one night...

The story began in an occult setting.

It was set at the end of the nineteenth century. There were rumors that a ghost had taken up residence in the Paris Opera House.

The ghost was called the "Phantom of the Opera," and he made various demands on the owners.

To pay him 240,000 francs a year, for example.

To leave the fifth box on the second floor open for him at every performance.

To put Christine Daaé onstage as a stand-in for the prima donna, Carlotta.

Christine had been only a lowly chorus girl, but she garnered an amazing success on that stage. The audience was intoxicated by her miraculous voice and erupted in applause.

In fact, Christine had been receiving secret instruction from an unidentified voice that she called the "Angel of Music."

The innocent young man who has loved Christine since they were children, Viscount Raoul de Chagny, listens in on her talking to the Angel of Music.

He feels a strident jealousy at her devotion to her instructor, the Angel of Music.

Christine loved the Angel of Music. He was seducing her, trying to lure her away!

Raoul's feelings were described in detail—his heart burning, toying with a simmering impulse, nearly frantic. Before I realized it, I was so absorbed in the story that my palms were sweating, and I felt an unease that seemed to press down on my chest.

That other Christine—Yuka Mito—was she all right?

Mito was taking lessons from an Angel of Music, too. She'd talked as if intoxicated about how the angel was taking her higher. And Mito's voice, like Christine's, had made amazing progress. But Mito hadn't revealed the name or true nature of her angel even to her best friend, Kotobuki.

Why was that? Because the angel had stopped her?

Or did Mito herself not know the truth about the angel?

Who could Mito's angel possibly be? And then, *who is Mito's Raoul?*

I recalled something Kotobuki had said on the way home.

"I think Yuka might be with the angel. Ever since she met the angel, Yuka's started turning me down a lot when I text her to go do stuff, and it seemed like it was because she wanted to sing with the angel as long as she absolutely could every day. When I told her it was like she'd gotten wrapped up in some weird religion, she got really upset and didn't text me for three whole days. I think she believes everything the angel tells her, and I think if he ordered her to do something, she would. No matter what it was..."

My heart skipped at the word *religion*. In Mito's eyes, the angel had the place of an infallible religious leader, and apparently Kotobuki had been concerned about her attachment to him this whole time. She may have also felt jealous that her best friend had been swept up in something that she didn't understand.

"You said Mito has a boyfriend, right? Are he and the angel the same person?" I thought I remembered her shouting something like that when Mr. Mariya invited her to that concert.

"No, Yuka started dating her boyfriend last fall, so he's different. He's from our school, and Yuka said she met him at the culture fair, but..."

Her voice broke off.

"Yuka wouldn't tell me his name. She would just play it off and promise to tell me about him after I got a boyfriend, and then laugh...I pushed it pretty hard, and eventually she gave me hints, but I didn't really understand them."

"What were they?"

"There were three of them. She told me there are nine people in his family, when he's thinking about something he has a habit of walking restlessly around his desk, and he really likes coffee."

Those were definitely tough. He liked coffee—well, there were a ton of people like that, and a person wouldn't notice the habit of walking around his desk unless he or she was pretty close to him. Families of nine were rare nowadays, but it would still be tough to sift through all the people at school for that information.

Kotobuki looked like she was flagging, too. But after a blank look crossed her face momentarily, it seemed that she had remembered something vital and she spoke up.

"Actually, the last time I talked to Yuka on the phone, she said her boyfriend was with her."

"When was the last time you talked to her?"

"Maybe...ten days ago?"

"Right about the time that she started having unexcused absences from school."

"Yeah...that day there was something I wanted to talk to Yuka about, and I got her voice mail. Later she sent me a message saying she'd call that night since she needed to get to her job. But then it was after midnight. When I still hadn't heard from her, I gave up and went to sleep. Whenever that happened before, Yuka would always send a message saying she couldn't call, so I thought it was strange. Then, after two in the morning, I suddenly got this call from Yuka. I was surprised and picked it up. She was in a really good mood, and she said, 'I'm with my boyfriend right now.'"

The wind ruffled Kotobuki's bangs, and she hunched her shoulders, looking cold.

"She woke me up, so I don't really remember that clearly, but she was rambling about how pretty the Christmas tree was and how warm she felt with her boyfriend's arms around her and stuff like that. She was weirdly worked up, too, and I thought that was strange."

Raoul was at our school.

Did Mito's boyfriend know that his girlfriend was missing? According to Kotobuki, the two of them were together right before she went missing.

In which case, wouldn't that mean that Mito's boyfriend was the one who knew where she was and not the angel?

The other thing that stuck out at me was the fact that Mito had continued to send messages to Kotobuki even after she disappeared.

The last time Kotobuki had received a phone call from Mito was ten days ago. From that day on, Mito had been absent from school. But even after that, the two of them kept sending text messages to each other like they always did. Was there some reason that Mito didn't want Kotobuki to find out about her disappearance?

And Mito's messages had broken off three days ago... What was she up to now?

My brain was strained to its limit. A roar started up in my ears, and I lay back on my bed. I rested the open book on my chest and let out a shallow breath.

There was too much I didn't understand.

If Tohko were here...

That nosy, thoughtless, slovenly, but still sensitive to odd stuff book girl with the kind eyes—I wondered how she would interpret this story.

"Maybe I should call her."

I turned my head to the side and gazed at the cell phone on my desk, then felt an ache brush over me, deep in my heart.

"I still haven't told her my phone number or e-mail address..."

Tohko didn't have a cell phone. She was an incurable dud with machines, so even if I gave her my e-mail, she'd probably never use it.

But that was an excuse, and right now I wanted to hear her warm, carefree voice more than anything.

But no! Tohko was studying for her exams, so I couldn't get her involved. This was Tohko, after all; obviously she would stick her nose in way too far if I told her about it.

My heart ached, and I tore my eyes from the phone, gripping my sheets tightly.

That's right—in the spring, Tohko would graduate and then leave...

My phone suddenly rang, almost stopping my heart.

It couldn't be Tohko, could it?!

I ran over to the desk and quickly checked who was calling. It was Akutagawa.

"Hey, Inoue?"

"Hey...what's up?"

"Oh, I'm just calling about Kotobuki. Things seemed pretty crazy so I was worried. Nothing's bothering you?"

That concern was typical of Akutagawa.

My tension eased, and my voice naturally softened. I thought how glad I was I'd become friends with him.

"Thanks. I'm fine. And I think Kotobuki made up with Mori and the others."

"Ah. If there's anything I can do to help, let me know. Doesn't matter how minor. Don't hesitate."

"Okay. Thanks."

The next day when I saw Akutagawa in class, my eyes bugged out.

"How'd you get those cuts?!"

He had claw marks running down his right cheek and neck. The three lines on his neck looked pretty deep and had puffed up purple and painful looking.

"It was just a cat...y'know."

Akutagawa smiled ruefully and looked away slightly.

"That looks like it hurts a lot! You okay?"

"Yeah. No big deal."

He turned his eyes away ever so slightly again.

"That's a pretty violent cat. But wait—does your family even have a cat?"

I'd been to his house a couple times, but there had just been koi swimming in the garden pond. I hadn't seen any cats...

"No...it's a neighbor's cat. I guess I was too rough with it and ticked it off."

His gaze shifted around restlessly, and he spoke as if he was holding something clamped between his back teeth.

Then out of nowhere, his face turned serious and he looked straight at me and asked, "But what about you? Everything still good?"

"We just saw each other yesterday. And you even called me. Oh, thanks for that, by the way."

"Oh, it was no problem...You didn't get any weird calls or texts after that, though? I mean, I hear people have been getting a lot of calls like that lately."

"So far, I haven't even gotten random hang ups."

Akutagawa leaned in even closer.

"Planning to change your phone number or e-mail?"

"No…what's going on, Akutagawa?"

My question seemed to bring him back to his senses, and he drew back, a forced-looking smile coming over his face.

"Well, if nothing's bothering you, it doesn't matter. Don't worry about it."

That was weird. *What's going on?* I wondered suspiciously, but I had my hands full with Kotobuki and I couldn't pursue anything else.

After school, we met up with some of Mito's classmates at the café from the day before.

They'd been surprised at how suddenly Mito's singing had improved, too.

"She got picked for the lead out of a *ton* of other girls. Turandot is a cruel, arrogant princess, which isn't Mito's image at *all*."

"The male lead, Calaf, is being played by Ogiwara, this young pro who's a huge star. In the scene where Turandot asks her questions, people were bad-mouthing Mito and saying her voice paled next to Ogiwara's and sounded like it was a total wreck."

But then when rehearsals had started, Mito's voice had enough energy to overwhelm the professional singer's.

"Mito kept it a secret, but she must've been getting lessons from a superfamous teacher. Otherwise she'd never get a voice like that so fast. They're even saying that the reason she's out now is that she's getting secret training somewhere."

"I guess I can see why she wouldn't step down from the role. There've been rumors about someone awesome backing her for a long time and that it was that person who got her picked for the lead," said another girl.

"Do you know who that person is?"

"No clue."

They shook their heads. Then as if suddenly remembering, one of them said, "Oh, but I saw Mito get into a car with a man in a black suit before! He had his arm around her, and it looked really fishy, and he called her 'Camellia'…"

After leaving the café, Kotobuki and I walked side by side down the street lit by white and gold Christmas lights.

We talked in spurts.

"Is Camellia a nickname? Do you know, Kotobuki?"

"Nope. I don't think anyone's ever called Yuka 'Camellia.' But maybe Yuka really is with the angel. The whole time she's been out of school, I was still getting messages from her that sounded like she was taking lessons from the angel. The man who called her Camellia might be the angel."

Kotobuki's expression was grim. It seemed like she felt seriously hostile toward the Angel of Music, and she seemed to believe that her best friend's disappearance was linked entirely to him.

In *Phantom of the Opera*, it was the Phantom who abducted Christine, taking her to his underground kingdom by pretending to be an angel and wearing a mask to hide his ugliness, so I could understand why she felt that way.

But was Mito really with the angel as Kotobuki said?

She had been with her boyfriend the night before she disappeared, so I couldn't say for certain.

Where exactly had Mito gone? Why didn't she come back to the dorms?

She still hadn't sent any new messages to Kotobuki.

The cool air ran over my skin with a prickly chill. The sky was cloudy, and I couldn't see the moon or stars; man-made lights were the only illumination on the street. An upbeat Christmas song played, clashing with our mood.

The expression in Kotobuki's eyes became vulnerable, and she said, "I feel like I've become Raoul. I'm jealous of Christine and the Phantom, and I keep wavering, but even if I go to save Christine from the Phantom who's kidnapped her, I won't do any good…"

"There are a lot of protagonists like that."

"Isn't the Phantom the protagonist of *Phantom of the Opera*?"

"I'm only partway through it, but since the story develops from Raoul's perspective, I feel like it's him."

"But the second half is a monologue by a mysterious Persian."

"It is?!"

"Raoul falls right into the Phantom's trap. There's nothing good about him."

"Hmm…"

Kotobuki pursed her lips and whispered sadly, ruefully, "Raoul really is useless."

"But I'm rooting for him," I told her with a smile. "I keep reading the story, thinking how great it would be if he rescued Christine and got a happy ending."

Kotobuki jerked her head up to look at me. She immediately buried her face in her scarf again and muttered shyly, "H…hmph. I see."

She was cute when she turned away and blushed, and my mouth curved into a smile despite itself.

Without turning back, Kotobuki muttered, "Um…yesterday, I was going through my old letters and I found a postcard Yuka sent me one summer from her mom's parents' house. It had an address on it. I'm thinking of sending a letter there. I might be able to contact Yuka's family."

I smiled.

"Yeah, that's a good idea. It'd be nice to find out where Mito is soon."

My angel always sings alone.

Beneath the moon, standing in the rustling grass, his melancholy voice reverberating across the indigo sky.

Even though my angel hates hymns, his voice is filled with a mournfulness and pleading that tears at my heart. I'm sure my angel thinks of someone who's gone while he sings. To comfort the soul of someone I don't know.

Long ago, my angel killed someone. He said bright red blood, like when you smash a strawberry, dyed the blue sheets and dripped onto the floor.

That after that, many people died for him.

My angel's name was blackened, his wings stained with blood, and he could no longer stay in the daylight world.

I felt awful.

I felt awful for my angel.

I always cry in front of him. But he never cries. He puts an arm around my shoulders, strokes my hair, and smiles for me.

Even when I tell him he can cry, he says he has nothing to be sad about and the tears won't come. He says he's never once cried in his entire life.

And so he won't sing me hymns, but he does sing lullabies for me.

So that I don't have scary dreams; so that I can forget everything painful and bitter that's happened and sleep soundly; so that tomorrow when I'm in the sunlight, I can hide my sins and smile purely, like every other perfectly ordinary girl.

The reason I can be his girlfriend and be Nanase's best friend is because my angel sings for me. If he didn't, I would be ashamed of how dirty and ugly I am. I would be paralyzed, and I wouldn't have anywhere near enough courage to stand before either of them.

Even though my angel has forgiven me and rescued me, who on earth will save him, who cannot be allowed into the light of the sun, who has lost his name, who can only hide himself in the world of darkness?

———

I was going to the music room to tell Mr. Mariya that we would be taking a break from organizing papers for a while when I found him smack in the middle of a love scene.

The petite girl whose lips were locked with his shrieked and scrambled away from him.

Then she shouted, "E-excuse me!" in an adorable voice, hung her head, and flew out of the room.

"...Mr. Mariya, what was that?"

Appearing at such a critical juncture had left me dazed, but Mr. Mariya smiled at me shamelessly.

"Ha-ha-ha. I think you ought to knock when you go into a room, Konoha."

"I did. And I think when you're doing stuff like that at school, you should keep an eye on your surroundings."

"Oh, absolutely true. Next time I'll be careful. She was an aggressive girl, and things just..."

Mr. Mariya wiped away his sweat with a handkerchief.

"Oh, is Nanase working at the library today?" he asked.

"Actually...I don't think we can help you right now."

I gave him the short version of how Kotobuki's best friend had disappeared.

"I see. That's awful," Mr. Mariya murmured, furrowing his brow, full of sympathy. Then he said something unexpected.

"Nanase's friend is that Yuka Mito girl who's playing Turandot at the recital, no? I met her a few times when I went to Shirafuji to mentor. She lacked a little polish, but there was something about her that shone. She seemed like the kind of girl who would grow with a good mentor. I was looking forward to hearing her Turandot. I had no idea whatsoever that such a thing had happened to her... That's too bad."

"Do you have any ideas about who Mito might have been taking lessons from? Apparently she called him her Angel of Music."

Mr. Mariya's face hardened suddenly, and he clasped his hands together firmly. The heavy-looking watch glinted on his left wrist.

"Her Angel of Music..."

"Yes. Have you heard of it?"

He slowly let out a breath and unlocked his fingers, then looked at me apologetically.

"No. I wasn't that close with Mito. But I'll ask the musicians I know."

"Thank you very much."

I bowed my head.

"Oh, Ms. Shoko Kagami from Shirafuji said to ask how you were doing."

Mr. Mariya broke out into a grin.

"Oh, you met her? She's beautiful, isn't she? All the boys around me yearned for her. She has a strong, forceful voice, and she got typecast in roles like Carmen."

"Yes, she's very pretty. She said that you used to be a rising star."

"Ha-ha-ha. She's exaggerating. I'm nothing that special. I'm much better suited to teaching here casually," he countered lightly, his cheerful voice spilling over with brightness.

His breezy smile was so noble it made me feel wonderful.

"When things settle back down, we can come help again."

"I'll be here."

We gave our words of farewell, and then I left the room.

I was meeting up with Kotobuki in the library after that.

I closed the door to the music room and was walking down the hall when suddenly a hand shot out from around a corner and grabbed my shoulder.

I jumped and felt goose bumps rising at the sensation of fingers digging into my skin through the material of my uniform.

When I turned around, I saw that a boy of about my height with glasses and colorless hair was glaring at me with a biting gaze.

It was the boy who had called me awful in the library before!

The world around me suddenly darkened, and I stiffened as if a maniac with a knife had appeared.

"Hey! What were you talking to Mariya about?"

"Who…are you?"

"That doesn't matter. Answer me. What did you say to him?"

I scowled at his imperious tone and shook his hand off.

"I don't need to answer to someone I don't know."

I turned my back on him and started to walk briskly away when a cold voice stabbed into me from behind.

"What a heartwarming scene."

The low voice was like the moaning of the wind that I'd heard in the stairwell, and the dark, bone-chilling gaze I'd felt that day came back to me, and all at once my skin prickled. When I turned around, jet-black eyes were glaring at me hatefully.

"Getting close to Mariya—I bet you get along. You're both hypocrites."

"What…are you talking about?"

"About you and Mariya. You're both living in pretty little

worlds and glossing over things with your smiles. You hurt others so you don't get hurt yourself."

I was staggered by this surreal situation, being relentlessly criticized by a stranger—I didn't even know his name—and my breathing grew more strained. His pointed gaze crawled over my face like a snake.

"You're always like that. You act like you're obtuse about Kotobuki, too, but aren't you really just playing off the fact that you're not into it? It's not that guys like you don't notice. You just don't want to know. You hate getting dirty, so even though you don't feel that way at all, you act nice and build up expectations, and I call people like that hypocrites."

Why did he hate me so much? Did he like Kotobuki? Did he dislike me because he had the wrong idea about us?

The thought crossed my mind, but the knives of his words overpowered it as they sliced into my chest, and the pain sent me reeling.

I was a hypocrite? It wasn't that I didn't notice. I just didn't want to know?

Even though I don't feel that way, I was acting nice and jerking Kotobuki around?

His words spun me around me like a pitch-black cutting wind and sliced into my flesh, sending up a spray of blood.

The back of my brain burned as if there were a fire pressing against it, and several times a lump rose in my throat, but it was uncontrolled and didn't form into words. I couldn't decide how to respond to his animosity—should I be angry, should I run, should I laugh it off?

Impaled by his piercing eyes, I stood immobilized as his funereal voice resounded in my ears.

"Don't go near Mariya again."

When he disappeared from sight, I was finally able to move again and sweat broke out all over my body.

What had just happened? Who *was* that guy?

And where did he get off telling me not to go near Mr. Mariya? I wanted to go back to the music room and put the screws to Mr. Mariya about it, but the guy was still nearby. I felt his dark eyes glaring at me and I got scared.

In the end, after all my hesitation, I went to the library.

Kotobuki worked busily behind the desk.

"Sorry. The other girl who's on duty was out today. Just give me a second."

"I'll be in the reading area, then."

"You look kind of spacey, Inoue."

"Nah, not really."

The guy's voice and glare still lingered in my mind. I couldn't talk to Kotobuki about it, about how I was jerking her around.

Just then, from somewhere nearby, I heard that same voice from moments ago.

"Kotobuki? I can take care of the rest. You can go home."

A student wearing glasses, surrounded by a somber air, appeared silently next to Kotobuki, and I shuddered.

"But you're not on duty today, Omi."

"There's not much left to do, so I can take over. There's someone waiting for you."

Kotobuki stole a glance at me.

I stood rooted to the spot, bloodcurdling thoughts running through my head.

"Well...I guess you can have the keys. Thanks, Omi."

"Sure. Bye."

He sent us off with a gruff look.

"Was that guy a first-year? What's his name?" I asked as we walked down the hall, desperately hiding how rattled I was.

"You mean Omi? His name's Shiro. Yeah, he's a first-year."

"I've never seen him at the library before. He works there, right?"

"Maybe 'cos he was out for the whole first semester. He's a little frail."

"...Are you guys friends?"

"What? Of course not. He's so quiet. Even when it's his shift, he hardly talks at all!"

She denied it fervently, her face red. When I saw how Kotobuki was acting, I remembered what Omi said to me and felt like my chest was being crushed.

"You're...glossing over things with your smile. You hurt others so you don't get hurt yourself."

"It's not that guys like you don't notice. You just don't want to know."

I remembered the way Kotobuki had looked at me when I'd gone to visit her at the hospital. And then the tears she'd shown me at rehearsal for the play...

"You may not remember it, but I...in middle school, I..."

"You...hate me. You won't be open with me."

"I'm sure you don't remember. But it meant a lot to me. So I went to see you again after that. Over and over, all through the winter. Every day."

Her words, her tears, that vulnerable look—what they had meant.

What Kotobuki had so desperately wanted to tell me—maybe I *had* been refusing to think about it.

Because for me, there was only one girl in the world, only Miu, and I would never be able to love like that again, focusing all of my emotions on someone.

I couldn't have strong feelings like that for anyone but Miu.

But then wasn't it cruel to be with Kotobuki like this?

Kotobuki was sad about the disappearance of her best friend, so wasn't my desire to help nothing but smug hypocrisy because I didn't want to be a bad person? If the worst should happen, was I prepared to help Kotobuki with her pain?

As I thought these things over, they dug into my chest, and it felt like they would knock the breath out of me.

Even though I could feel Kotobuki torturously stealing glances at me as I gritted my teeth, my face tense, it didn't change anything. It took everything I had to talk about the weather, my words horribly wooden—"Sure is cold today"—and I just felt awkward.

By the time we reached Mito's house, we were both completely silent.

The nameplate had toppled off the wall, the lights were out, and the house was now completely abandoned.

I knew Kotobuki was grasping at straws, thinking that if she came here, maybe she would discover something. But the bleak sight that assaulted us eradicated even that paltry hope. The mail cascading out of the mailbox had been exposed to the weather and grown tattered, and the glass in one of the windows facing the yard was broken. In the midst of a perfectly ordinary neighborhood, this was the only house that stood like a graveyard.

Kotobuki took unsteady steps through the front gate and rang the doorbell.

There was no answer.

Next she pounded on the door with a fist—again and again, gritting her teeth, tears beading at the corners of her eyes.

Still she didn't hear the voice she'd hoped to from behind the door.

"Forget it. You're going to hurt your hands."

I grabbed her hands from behind to stop her. My own heart felt like it was ripping apart.

At the same time, the word *hypocrite* tumbled through my mind and threatened to knock me to the ground.

Kotobuki turned her back on me, hung her head, and wept softly.

Kotobuki was silent until she got home.

She stopped in front of a three-story building and murmured, her voice barely audible, "This is it." There was a sign for a dry cleaner's store on the first floor.

"So your family are dry cleaners, huh?"

She nodded and again murmured, "My grandma does it." She had stopped crying at least, but her eyes were bright red and she was sniffling.

"Is it okay that you're so late coming home?"

"It's fine. Um...I'm—I'm sorry about what happened," she said, her voice hoarse, and then she went up the stairs to the second floor.

She looked down at me from there with a terribly fragile expression.

She looked like she wanted to say something, but she didn't say it. Her face fell slightly, and she disappeared behind the door.

The instant our eyes met, I thought I saw guilt surface in Kotobuki's face.

That feeling swirled around inside me in a pitch-black mass and made it hard for me to breathe.

"You're both hypocrites."

"You hate getting dirty, so even though you don't feel that way at all, you act nice and build up expectations."

It happened just as I was starting to walk down the dark, freezing road to go home.

I saw the shadow of a person standing on the other side of the street. It looked like he was staring at the door Kotobuki had just disappeared behind.

The clouds covering the sky broke, and moonlight illuminated his profile for just an instant.

Omi?!

Just as I was trying to get another look, the shadow turned its back and started walking.

I followed quickly after him. That *was* Omi, wasn't it? What was he doing there? Had he been following us?

At that thought, the hair on my back stood on end and a chill came up through my legs.

The shadow walked steadily on.

Following him, my own steps grew quicker. My breathing became strained, and I panted more. My warm, cloudy white breath caressed my cold cheeks.

Before I realized it, I was standing frozen in a pitch-dark alley that the light of the streetlamps didn't reach.

The shadow became one with the darkness, and I couldn't find a shape that looked like Omi anywhere.

No—but I was sure he had turned this corner! Where did he disappear to?!

In my confusion, I heard a sudden, furtive singing.

It was a low voice that sounded like it was weeping.

A voice like a ghost's filled with bitterness and sorrow.

What the—?! Where was this voice coming from?! In front of me? No, behind me? No, from over there? No, it wasn't there—it was from over there. No, not there, either!

The voice seemed to be echoing from every direction, one after another, and gripped by the terror that was crawling up my spine, I stood frozen.

Hadn't there been a scene like this in *Phantom of the Opera*?

Raoul, who had gone into the shadowy kingdom below the opera house to rescue Christine, is bewildered by the illusions made by the Phantom, and he descends into madness.

This voice did not belong to a person.

It was the voice of an angel! The voice of a monster! It was the dirge of the masked man who lived straddling heaven and earth—the Phantom!

It dug its fingers into my soul, and I lost all composure at the diabolical singing that slowly closed in around me. My throat burned, I couldn't breathe, and my fingertips started to get numb.

Oh no—I was having an attack.

These had plagued me often after Miu jumped off the roof, and sweat broke out over my entire body, as if the Phantom's voice had called it forth. My head whirled, and hoarse, reedy breaths escaped my throat.

My knees buckled, and I fell to my knees on the cold pavement.

The singing became a sly chuckle. It sounded like a man's voice, like a woman's voice, like a young boy's laugh, and like a young girl's laugh.

Inside of my eyelids rose the image of Miu, wearing a middle school uniform and her hair pulled back in a ponytail, and she turned to me with an empty smile, then fell away backward.

That image repeated again and again like a kaleidoscope.

"It's not that you don't notice."

"You just don't want to know."

A voice flecked with poison accused me.

"You're just pretending not to see it. You hurt her and chased her to her death. You're a murdering hypocrite."

No—no—no.

My entire body quaked, and the intervals between my breaths grew markedly shorter.

Miu fell away.

Fell away—

After a little while, I guess I lost consciousness.

When the ring of my cell phone woke me, I was lying on my stomach, my arms and legs thrown out, in a dark alley that smelled like rotting food.

A lighthearted Western song I liked played from the pocket of my coat.

I lifted my stiff body and got out my phone with frozen, numb hands and looked at the screen.

Ryuto...

"Oh, Konoha. You got a computer on where you are?"

Ryuto said it out of nowhere in a hurried manner.

"Sorry, I'm outside. I'll get back in about an hour, though," I answered, resting a hand on the wall of the alley as I got to my feet unsteadily.

Feeling was slowly returning to my skin and to my heart. Had that singing been a bad dream? I felt like I was standing on the boundary between illusion and reality, and my mind was still a little clouded.

"Oh. Then I'll send ya the file. Take a look when you get home."

"What did you find?"

"I actually tried lookin' for Yuka Mito a little myself. I thought

I might be buttin' in, but if ya don't solve your problems before Christmas Eve, that's bad news for me."

Ryuto dropped a bomb that blew away the cottony mist billowing up inside my brain with that one.

"Yuka's been on a members-only site since this summer under the name Camellia. She's got customers there. Looks like she mighta been an underage escort."

As soon as I opened the door to my room, I started up my computer without even changing my clothes first and opened the file Ryuto had sent me. The homepage of a shady website trooped down the screen, along with a user agreement and girls' profiles.

Ryuto had told me, *"They noticed the unauthorized access and locked me out partway through, so I couldn't see everythin'.*

"The Camellia that's number sixteen on that list is Yuka."

I felt a fraying anxiety rising up in my chest, and holding my breath, I scrolled down the screen.

No. 16 Name: Camellia.

The instant my eyes fell on those words, my throat clamped tight and I felt dizzy.

The words of Mito's classmates resurfaced in my mind, alongside a numbing pain.

"I saw Mito get into a car with a man in a black suit before! He had his arm around her, and it looked really fishy, and he called her Camellia."

No...it had to be a coincidence!

No matter how I denied it, my anxiety remained, and my heart pounded almost painfully fast.

I read through the profile without so much as blinking. The occupation field said, "I'm a high school girl at the S Music

Academy," and the comments field said, "I want to be an opera singer. I'm looking for a nice old man who'll hold me tenderly."

Sweat broke out, soaking the hand that gripped the mouse. Was this really Mito?

There was no denying it—this was an illegal dating service. Had Mito been soliciting men for an underage escort service here? Had she made money by meeting with anonymous hordes of men?

I followed the words on the screen even farther, hunched over the computer intently.

Hobbies: Listening to classical music, shopping

Favorite food: Strawberries

Favorite place to go on a date: Theme park

Favorite author: Miu Inoue

Miu Inoue?!

I felt as if I'd been punched in the head.

Thrust suddenly upon my spirit, which was already strained to its breaking point, the name gave me a shock that bore exponentially more force than usual.

I grew feverish, as if my entire body was engulfed in a blazing fire, and my thoughts came to a complete halt.

Her favorite author was Miu Inoue.

Her name was Camellia.

It had never ended. I was still lying in the alley and had never woken up. What was this nightmare?

⟢◆⟣

It's not true! It's not!

Dad! Mom! Satoshi! Why?! Why did you do that?!

It isn't true, is it? We talked on the phone about me going home for New Year's and spending the time together! You said you were both working hard, so I shouldn't push myself, that I should cut back on my job since the recital was coming up and I should take care of my throat so I didn't get sick. You said you'd send me the dried persimmons I like so much. That you wanted to see me soon, that it would be wonderful to live together as a family again. That it would be all right definitely someday. You both laughed! You said Satoshi had made friends at his new school and was having fun. That I should keep working on my singing.

So then why?! Satoshi was still in middle school!

I worked so hard so that we could live together.

The first time I met a customer, they told me all I had to do was eat dinner and talk a little, but then they took me to a hotel and did that to me, and I was mortified, scared, hurt; it was awful.

It was like I'd been stained black, and I couldn't look anyone in the eyes anymore, and whenever I thought of how I would have to keep living in fear, keeping this a secret, it made my head spin, and I wished I could die.

I threw up in the bathroom so many times. I scrubbed at my body with soap and a towel until my skin was raw, but the memory that *I did that* never faded.

Even so, I'd gotten money. I thought that with that money, Dad wouldn't have to get beaten up by those loan collectors or have to grovel to them, that we could pay for Satoshi's school, too.

That was the only thing I could do. I thought it would be okay if I stopped being normal, as long as we could all live together and be happy like before.

There were a lot of gross customers after that, too, and I was really miserable and nauseated, and every day it was like a little sliver was carved away from the edges of myself, and foul-smelling black muck gradually piled up on my body, and I thought I was going to be buried in it, that eventually I would be exposed, and all I could do was flinch.

When there was a story on the news about the arrest of police officers who had engaged underage escorts, Nanase told me, "I can't believe those girls, either. They're just sixteen! I'd never be able to do that with someone I didn't care about." I thought my heart would stop.

When he held me, it hurt me and I felt guilty, and I accidentally pushed him away and made him sad.

But whenever I think about how I'm doing it for you guys, I can tell myself it's still okay.

And besides, there was an angel with me. I got to meet an angel.

So even if it was torture, it was fine. I could bear it.

I can't sing hymns anymore, either!

I can't believe in God!

Even if I only pray to have my heart made pure, it accomplishes nothing. God will not smile on my corruption. He's chased me into a world of darkness.

In any case, I'll probably lose him and Nanase.

Did my angel experience such despair?

I have to sing. I have nothing left but that so that I'll stay on my feet and not choose death when he and Nanase leave me.

I mustn't cry! Sing! Keep singing!

Not a song praising the Lord, but a song calling for battle.

Chapter 3—The Angel Watches from the Shadows

The next morning, when I ran into Kotobuki in the classroom, she greeted me curtly.

"Morning."

Her eyes were still red, and she was acting awkward. But I may have been just as strained as her.

"Morning, Kotobuki..."

Yuka Mito was an underage escort.

Did I need to tell Kotobuki that?

A bitter lump rose in my throat, and I failed to find anything I could say next. But then Kotobuki hesitantly held a bundle of papers out to me.

"These are copies of Yuka's messages... You said yesterday you wanted to see them."

"Th-thanks."

"It's just the most recent ones, and I...deleted all the personal stuff..."

She looked down, troubled, and fumbled for words.

"I'm just giving them to you in case, but if you don't read them, that's fine, too."

"No, I will."

Our fingers brushed slightly as I took the copies from her, and Kotobuki flinched.

That made my chest squeeze with pain again.

Should I be staying so close to her? I still didn't have an answer to that.

The truth jabbed at me anew, mercilessly pursuing me, crushing my throat tight.

I struggled to get my uneven breathing under control and asked, "Hey, did you ever ask Mito what her job was?"

"She worked at a family restaurant. Her shifts were at night, so she would gripe about the gross customers she got sometimes."

"...Oh. Do you know what restaurant it was?"

"Nope. Yuka told me not to come 'cos she was embarrassed. If I'd known this was going to happen, I wish I'd asked her about it, though."

Kotobuki bit her lip.

"Well..."

There was a hitch in my throat that made it hard to talk. Was I managing to look calm? My face wasn't tense, was it?

"What sorts of books did Mito read usually?"

"Huh?"

Kotobuki looked up, suspicious.

"I don't have any big reason for asking. I was just wondering if there was anything in particular besides *Phantom of the Opera*..."

She must have thought it was a weird question. There was puzzlement in her eyes.

"She liked foreign children's stories...She read those a lot. *Little House on the Prairie* or *Little Women*...Oh, she also liked *Sarah, Plain and Tall.*"

What about Miu Inoue?

It got as far as the back of my throat, and then I swallowed it.

Last night the name that I'd seen on the computer—Camellia—

and the words that listed her favorite author as Miu Inoue had plastered themselves inside my head like a curse.

Miu's book had been read mainly by teens and twentysome-things and had become a record-breaking best seller, and its movie and TV show had both become hits as well. Even if Mito did read Miu, it wasn't so unusual. It must have just been a coincidence.

Even so, I couldn't help but react to that ill-fated name that had taken everything from me.

I desperately composed myself and said, "This feels pretty different from *The Phantom of the Opera*. Actually, I haven't had the time to finish it yet. Right now I'm at the part where Raoul sets off underground the opera house to rescue Christine."

"...Oh," Kotobuki responded listlessly. Then she turned her gaze down, as if conflicted, and bit her lip, then mumbled, "I...wonder if maybe Raoul never existed. That maybe all that stuff about a boyfriend was just in Yuka's imagination."

Surprised, I asked, "Why do you think that?"

She fiddled restlessly with her nails in her lap, and then Kotobuki replied in a gloomy voice.

"Because it wasn't normal...the fact that she wouldn't tell me his name, but there were a bunch of times that it seemed like she was happy and gushing about him. But then all of a sudden she seemed like she didn't want to talk, or like it hurt her to say anything more. It was especially bad lately...It was like she didn't want me to ask about him. And then these last two months or so, whenever I was talking to Yuka on the phone, another call would come in almost every time..."

"From her boyfriend?"

"Yeah."

Kotobuki frowned.

"Then Yuka would say, 'Sorry, it's my boyfriend. I'll text you later.' Then she'd hang up. But she didn't used to act that way. I guess he didn't like her working in a restaurant at night because it was too dangerous. Then Yuka told me that he would get worried and call her. It was like he was stalking her..."

Something ominous slowly filled my heart.

Maybe he'd learned of Mito's secret.

Then he might not have been able to stop himself from calling her all the time to check what she was doing...

Or if he was a product of Mito's imagination as Kotobuki suggested, then might those calls have been from Mito's "job"...?

"...But the last time you talked to Mito on the phone, didn't she tell you that she was looking at a Christmas tree with him?"

A dark shadow fell over Kotobuki's eyes, and her tone grew hard.

"That's true...But she was weirdly excited then, and I thought she sounded like she was acting onstage."

In the deep of a night fallen into silence, had Mito been talking to Kotobuki all alone on the other end of the phone?

She was with him now...

When I imagined that, a shudder went through me, as if a paintbrush had run along the back of my neck.

"He may have actually been there. But I thought maybe things had stopped going well for them and they'd broken up...that maybe she couldn't say it and was pretending they were still going out. When I remember talking to Yuka, that's how it seemed.

"It's only my personal theory, though," Kotobuki murmured with difficulty.

Yes—none of this was more than conjecture.

Had Mito had a boyfriend or not? And what about the angel and her secret lessons?

There was still no proof that she had been working as an escort under the name Camellia, either.

Even though I knew that was a cop-out, it was what I told myself, and I decided not to say anything to Kotobuki about it yet.

"You just don't want to know."

I argued desperately against the voice echoing in my head.
That's not true! I just don't want to hurt Kotobuki. Besides, was there any reason to try to force the truth out? That might cause something worse. If you could avoid hurting anyone, that was better by far.

The school bell rang, and we all returned to our seats.

Akutagawa furrowed his brow and looked at me worriedly.

I got your message, Nanase.
Sorry, I've got a lesson after work that day. Would next Saturday work?

Omigosh, Nanase! I wasn't paying attention and I gained five pounds! My angel says it's better to be fat, to up your lung power, but it's still such a shock. Starting today, I'm having an apple and soy cookies for lunch!

Today, I sang the aria for the Queen of the Night in The Magic Flute in front of everyone.
Even I was shocked at how long I stretched my voice out, and the teachers were surprised, too. The kids in class were asking which of the great singers I was getting lessons from, so I told them it was an Angel of Music and their jaws all hit the floor. It was so funny.

Even though it's the truth.

Someone said something mean to me at work. That customer is such a jerk!
But I have to put up with it to earn money for school.
Sigh...why is music so expensive? We have to pay for concert tickets for class and other stuff—it gives me such a headache.

Listen to this, Nanase! I got picked for the lead in our next recital! Hurray! Promise you'll come!

I can't make any time for dates with the rehearsals for the recital, so I think my boyfriend's a little unhappy. But he's a nice guy, so he tells me to keep up the hard work. I wish I could introduce him to you. And you should (*remainder deleted)

Understood—I'll leave Christmas open for you, my very best friend, Nanase.
Obviously I'll be with my boyfriend on Christmas Eve, though.
Heh-heh-heh, why don't you just take the initiative soon? It'll be fine! You're cute, so I'm sure. (*remainder deleted)

I made my ring tone a Christmas song.
It's "Santa Claus Is Coming to Town."
Too soon?

Until your love is realized, I'm keeping my boyfriend's name a secret.

If you want me to gush, though, I'll write as much as you could ever want.

Last year on Christmas Eve, we exchanged matching rings.

We promised we would always wear them, but he got teased at school when he wore it, so he took it off his finger and hid it.

Before a date, he gets it out real quick and slips it back on. I just love watching him do that from a little ways off.

And then! When he's sad, he squeezes my hand tight to get through it, or when I touch his hand and he loosens his grip just a little . . . I feel so sublime and indulgent, and I think, Wow, I love him so much.

When our rings touch each other, they make a noise, ching . . . that little sound is more beautiful to me than the most wonderful music.

Well? Are you jeeealous?

Hurry up and get a man, Nanase! Boyfriends are the best!

When you get a boy, we'll go on a double date.

Hey Nanase—I'm totally overjoyed right now, and singing makes me so happy I can't even stand it. With my angel beside me, I've gotten better and better, and I've started to like songs more.

You don't seem to like my angel, Nanase.

Whenever I talk about him, you get in a bad mood.

I get that you're worried about me, but when you say stuff like how he seems fishy or ask if he's tricking me, it makes me feel bad, too.

My angel is important to me and I care about him a lot.

> I had to work all of a sudden.
> Sorry. I'll call you later.
> Don't let it bug you too much. Mori and them will (*remainder deleted)
> See you later, Nanase.

Our fourth period classics class was independent study, so I quickly took care of my classwork, then read through Mito's messages.

Even when I'd read to the very last line, I couldn't see why Mito had disappeared, and she didn't talk very much about her boyfriend or the angel.

Just from reading the messages, she came off as a perfectly ordinary, cheerful girl...

The bell rang and lunch break began.

"I'm gonna go buy some bread from a stand. You go on ahead and start," Akutagawa said.

"Huh? But you always bring your lunch."

"My mom forgot to turn on the rice cooker."

Akutagawa and I shared this brief exchange, and then I went out into the hall where—

My cell phone vibrated in my pocket.

I had a new message, sender unknown.

I checked the message, then gulped.

> He's Lucifer.

What was this?

Spam?

I connected to the Internet on my phone to look up the word, and my jaw dropped.

Lucifer was the angel who had turned his back on God and been cast into hell—he was the king of hell.

My breathing became suddenly strained.

An angel of music and the fallen angel Lucifer—was this a coincidence? Or had there been some sort of purpose in sending this to me?

But who had done it?

Who did "he" refer to? Who was Lucifer?

The boy with the glasses and cold stare came to my mind. Could this be Omi harassing me? I didn't know how he'd gotten my address, but already it was the only possibility I could imagine. Besides, even ignoring what had happened yesterday, there was way too much I didn't know about him.

What should I do? Should I try asking Omi? But what if he said something to me again? What if he glared at me with that naked malice in his eyes?

Conflicted, I went to the library.

There was a different student working at the desk. My tension melted, and I sighed with relief. I was starting to head back to the classroom when I saw Omi at a table in the reading area reading a book.

My heart leaped into my throat.

What now, what now? Thoughts tearing at my belly, I held my breath and drew closer.

I peeked at his open book from behind, and instantly a spasm of horror shot down my spine.

My entire body was chilled immediately, as if someone had dumped cold water over my head.

It was a hardcover edition of Miu Inoue's book…

Why was he reading Miu's book of all things?!

Camellia's profile flashed before my eyes with perfect clarity. Could Omi know something about Mito? No, I was overthinking things.

I choked down a hard lump in my throat and called out to him.

"That's by Miu Inoue, right?"

Omi turned around. He saw my face, and his eyes narrowed behind his glasses' frames, as if disgusted by who had come visiting.

At first glance, he looked like any other modern boy, but there was unusual power in his gaze. My belly cramped, and sweat broke out on my palms. *Calm down.* He wasn't much bigger than me. He was just a regular boy who was younger than me, right?

"You like stuff like that?"

Omi answered in a frosty tone, "No, I hate it. This book and Miu Inoue, too."

His words sliced my chest open and slammed me against the floor of an abyss.

I couldn't move a muscle. He kept his sharp, venomous gaze fixed on me and went on spitefully. "It's tripe with nothing but amateur phrasing, like something an elementary school student would write, and there are sickeningly sweet word choices dripping all over every page. The main character's idiotic optimism and hypocrisy remind me exactly of a certain someone, and it pisses me off."

His eyes glinted like a feral dog's. His words were heavy with scorn.

They were the same as the words I'd spat out in front of the girls from my class once.

"What's so interesting about that book? The writing is bad, the composition is sloppy—it's like being forced to read a not-too-bright middle schooler's shallow poetry. It's laughable.

"Don't you think everyone just made a big deal out of it because a fourteen-year-old girl won the award?

"I hate Miu Inoue."

Yes, I thought the way you do absolutely. That a book like this is terrible and has no value whatsoever. That it was some kind of mistake that everyone was making a fuss over someone like me.

That I hated Miu Inoue more than anything in the world.

"I dunno how she wasn't ashamed to write about a pretty little world that's bright in every last crevice and spilling over with all this benevolence. The stuff this book talks about is nothing but lies. People like this— like Miu Inoue or Mariya or you—who can only see the surface of things or of other people's hearts, who believe the sun shines for them and that they can walk brazenly down the middle of the street, hurt people and force them into corners naively."

I'd never had Miu Inoue criticized to my face by another person before. I'd had no idea it would stab into my heart like this and hurt so unbearably. That it would affect me so much...

My steps faltered, and I almost fell over. Then I said, "Sorry for interrupting," and fled the library.

Even if it was pathetic, even if it was ignoble, I couldn't stand to be the object of his hate-filled gaze anymore, to be cut apart by the knives of his black words.

I knew better than anyone that Miu's book was nothing but lies.

Reality wasn't that kind or that beautiful; prayers and promises were nothing but dreams that passed by in a moment.

A peaceful life would be shattered all too easily, the couple who smiled at each other and interlaced their fingers would go their separate ways, and memories were nothing more than poison that dredged up turmoil.

I didn't know how to handle the fever and pain coursing through my body.

I hate Miu Inoue! The fact is, Miu Inoue and her book are both corrupt and caked with lies.

I know that! I *know*!

In the empty corridor, I rested my hand on the wall and took several shallow breaths. Cold sweat covered me, and a throbbing chill snaked through me, as if I had caught an evil cold.

Just as I was about to slump to the floor, someone touched my shoulder.

"Is something the matter, Inoue?"

When I turned around and looked up, I saw Mr. Mariya standing behind me, holding me up.

"Mr. Mariya..."

"You look awful. Do you want to go to the nurse's office?" he asked worriedly, knitting his brows.

I shook my head feebly. "I'm fine. I'll have it under control...soon..."

Mr. Mariya's brow furrowed even more deeply.

"You don't look like you'll be fine. If you don't want to go to the nurse, then let's go to the music room. Teacher's orders. Come with me."

"Here you go."

"Thank you."

The aroma of cinnamon wafted over to me in a white cloud of steam.

I accepted with both hands the hot chai that Mr. Mariya offered to me with a kind smile, then drank it sip by sip, blowing on it intermittently.

The music room was blindingly bright with light streaming in the window, and it was quiet and warm.

My breathing returned to normal and my sweat dried, but a chilling ache persisted inside my heart.

Mr. Mariya gazed at me with a gentle expression as he drank his own chai, and then he asked, "What happened?"

I paused.

"It's all right if you don't want to talk about it."

"...Have you ever been hated, Mr. Mariya?"

"Did you have a fight with Nanase, then?"

My fingers tightened around the paper cup, and I hung my head, prompting Mr. Mariya to say quietly, "I have been hated, yes."

When I looked up, he was staring out the window, a melancholy expression on his face.

"My parents were musicians, so my whole life I've been expected to become a professional, and I never questioned that. But over time, my music stopped meshing with the voices around me...I was unable to reconcile myself very well with them and stopped caring about anything. I wanted to wipe out my name and the life that was mine. At the time, I nursed such thoughts every day."

I watched Mr. Mariya's face in profile and listened to his sorrowful voice.

Mr. Mariya rested a hand gently on the heavy-looking watch around his wrist, and a placid yet somehow mournful smile came over his face. He murmured, "I suppose that's why I became a teacher and why I'm here. So that I wouldn't have to hate myself."

Mr. Mariya might have found it torture to be called a genius and to be treated specially...like I'd shuddered every time Miu Inoue was celebrated on TV or in the papers.

"Which reminds me, has Mito been found?"

"No...we only have a clue about the Angel of Music."

"I see..."

As my eyes clouded over, Mr. Mariya's voice became tinged with gloom once again, and he murmured, "It may be best if you don't look for her anymore."

"Why?" I asked, startled.

"If Mito went into hiding of her own volition, perhaps she doesn't wish to be found."

Shoko had said that when he was still in school, Mr. Mariya had disappeared one day out of the blue.

Maybe he was remembering that. His voice was rough and frail.

"The truth doesn't always help people. There are some things people are happier not knowing.

"People who dream of being artists in particular...they're all very cowardly and have no confidence and are easy to influence. While they're praised for their talent, they're up against a wall, and it's hard, so hard, and there are no options left for them...Even so, I've seen a fair number of people who can't give up, and their hearts grow sick. I really do wonder why they need to be pushed so far. Talent is a very dubious thing, and there has never been and will never be a clear way to measure it. The illusion of talent can at times be a weapon to hurt people. Even though beautiful music is equal for its listeners, it's not like that for those who bring it into being. And their talent can't continue forever.

"Even a singer who was called an angel, who burned brilliantly, immersed in the people's praise, is forgotten now...He doesn't sing anymore."

When he said the word *angel*, a fierce pain came into Mr. Mariya's eyes.

"Why did the angel stop singing?"

Mr. Mariya murmured sadly, "Someone...died. An old musician slit his wrists while he listened to the angel's hymns."

I gasped at this shocking story, and Mr. Mariya went on with even more difficulty.

"The angel made people unlucky, caused their destruction. The angel's singing was filled with corruption and pushed many people to their deaths. So the angel doesn't sing anymore. He mustn't," Mr. Mariya declared, gripping his wrists. He looked as if he blamed himself.

Did the angel Mr. Mariya spoke of have something to do with Mito...?

And Mr. Mariya...no, could he himself be—

"He was our rising star."

"They said he could be a symbol of Japanese opera."

Mr. Mariya looked extremely tired, but he sucked in a breath, as if shaking something off, and picked up the paper cup he had set down on the table.

Then he looked at me and faintly, sadly he smiled.

"You know, Inoue, success is a fleeting thing for an artist. Personally, I choose to have this cup of chai instead."

———⋇———

I wonder what Miu Inoue is like...

Sometimes I picture her as I turn the pages.

A weekly magazine wrote that she might be a rich sophisticate, but I think Miu is a regular girl. That she's a happy, ordinary girl with a family, friends, and a person that she likes.

A wonderful girl who's surely kind and innocent and always laughing...

I like Miu's book because it has a ton of pretty photos in it instead of illustrations.

Photos of blue skies, open fields, rain, a pool, a gymnasium, a water fountain, a chin-up bar...perfectly ordinary and yet nostalgic things.

Also loving feelings, a faithful heart, an important promise. It fills my heart with beautiful, pure stuff.

I wish you would read Miu, too, Nanase.

I know you'd love it, but before when I told you, "Miu Inoue's the same age as us. I wonder what she's like," you sulked and said, "If she won't show her face, she must be a dog."

You say awful things, Nanase, but you're not mean. You've never been the kind of girl to say stuff like that, though...

I hung your picture back up in the living room, Nanase. You're frowning a little in it, and you look so cute.

The whole wall is covered in pictures of my angel, you, and me. And then the blue roses.

As I gaze at them, I pray from my corruption.

That you'll be happy and be at peace, Nanase.

That you'll be surrounded by family and friends in the warm light of day to which I can't return and that you'll laugh from the heart.

That your love might come true at least.

I hope you'll have a love like Itsuki and Hatori's in Miu Inoue's novel.

———◆———

Mr. Mariya was hiding something from us.

With that woolly-headed thought in my heart, I went back to my classroom just before the bell rang.

"Sorry. I just started feeling sick, so I was resting in Mr. Mariya's office."

Akutagawa's brow furrowed. "You okay?"

"Yeah, I'm pretty much better."

"Oh. That's good then. I thought…"

Akutagawa faltered. He looked conflicted and then, just as he was about to say something to me—

"Nanase!"

I turned in surprise at Mori's voice and saw Kotobuki with her hands on her desk, her face ashen, shaking.

"Are you sick? Nanase?!"

I hurried over to her, too.

Something clattered by her feet. A familiar-looking cell phone had fallen to the floor.

Wait, that's not Kotobuki's, is it?

I bent down and picked it up and was starting to snap it closed when Kotobuki snatched it out of my hand with incredible force.

I was shocked at Kotobuki, her eyebrows high, panting roughly, tears pooling in her eyes, and trembling as she glared at me, but just then our teacher came into the room.

"Excuse me, Kotobuki looks kind of sick, so I'm going to take her to the nurse's office."

Mori left the room with Kotobuki leaning on her. Kotobuki gripped the phone fiercely to her chest. Her face, which was tense and seemed frightened about something, hung down.

What was going on with her? I had caught a glimpse of a long text message on the screen, and it was bugging me.

Could it be that someone had sent a strange message to Kotobuki's phone, too?!

Once the break started, I went to Mori's desk to ask how Kotobuki was doing.

She answered with a troubled look.

"Um…I don't really know, either, but she seems a little confused. She's talking about this 'Phantom' thing…"

I had a vision of a cold shadow falling across me, and sweat covered my palms.

"Phantom…she said that?"

"I might not've heard her right. But I think you should wait here until Nanase comes back."

My breathing became difficult, and my heart was constricted by anxiety.

So that message did have some kind of connection to the one I'd gotten, then. It had been about something so shocking that Kotobuki had dropped her phone.

It was after we'd finished cleanup that Kotobuki returned.

I watched, feeling frustrated, as Mori and the others surrounded her and started talking to her, chorusing, "We were so worried!" Kotobuki repeated something in an undertone to them with an awkward, forced-looking smile. When Kotobuki finally picked up her backpack and left the classroom, I chased after her. I called out to stop her in the hallway.

"Kotobuki!"

Her slender back twitched. But she didn't stop—she started walking quickly, as if to flee.

"Hold on, Kotobuki!"

I grabbed her arm, and she turned around with tears in her eyes.

"Let me go…!"

"What happened? What did the Phantom do?"

Fear ran plainly through her wide eyes. An array of complex emotions passed over her pale face—terror, confusion, pain, covetousness, sorrow.

What had happened? Why was she so afraid? And why did she look so sad…?

Struggling, Kotobuki knit her brows tightly, and in a trembling voice, she whispered, "It's nothing. Just leave me alone. I'll look for Yuka by myself, so I don't need you hanging around anymore…"

"But—"

I saw lucid tears gathering in Kotobuki's eyes, and I grew even more hesitant.

Looking as if she was holding up desperately under the trembling of her voice and tears, Kotobuki said, "I—I mean, come on…When we went to Yuka's house yesterday, you looked…like it was really hard on you…I hated seeing you like that! I can't handle it! I'm not even your girlfriend, but I'm putting you through all this…I'm sorry. Thanks for everything you've done so far. But please, just leave me alone."

My mind went white, as if I'd been socked out of nowhere, and all the strength went out of my hands.

Seeing my conflict had hurt Kotobuki as she stood beside me…

"Kotobuki?"

Omi appeared without the sound of a single footfall and spoke in a low voice.

"The librarian is looking for you. Could you come to the library?"

"…Okay," she murmured hoarsely before going away with Omi, her head hanging down.

As they were leaving, Omi turned back and pierced me with a cold, contemptuous gaze.

"*…Hypocrite.*"

My legs buckled, my throat tensed, and I couldn't utter a single word.

The part of me that wanted to help Kotobuki wasn't a lie. My heart had ached at how she was sobbing so feebly, and I'd wanted to help her somehow or other.

But it was being at her side halfheartedly that had caused her to look that pained.

It hurt to breathe, and I thought my throat might rip open. I wanted to erase the fact that I had ever lived. I had truly, truly not meant to hurt Kotobuki at all. This was exactly like that time in the library. I was an awful hypocrite just like Omi said.

I stumbled down the hall, feeling pathetic, as if everyone in the world was looking at me askance and criticizing me. My heart had been hollowed out. It burned with a fiery pain, and tears started to come to my eyes with the desolation and suffering of it all.

No. I can't cry. I don't have that right. How could I have made Kotobuki say something like that? She had looked like she was on the verge of tears.

I desperately blinked back the thoughts welling up in me.

What should I do now?

Kotobuki said she didn't want me involved anymore since she was going to search for Mito alone.

But I couldn't walk away from Kotobuki when she was in this state. Was it better to be with her even if I hurt her? Or should I go away for Kotobuki's sake? I didn't know.

Without realizing it, my legs took me to the familiar book club room at the western end of the third floor.

Even though Tohko wouldn't be there.

Her ghost would be enough.

I missed her.

I missed Tohko.

I turned the cold doorknob and opened the door to the room, and then I heard a gentle voice.

"Hello, Konoha."

Sitting on a fold-up chair by the window with her knees drawn up to her chest, flipping through a book, was the book girl, like a violet, her long, thin braids trailing to her hips.

Chapter 4—The Book Girl's Value

"Dickens's *A Christmas Carol* is like a meat loaf fresh out of the oven. It's got great texture, and even a child can chew their way through it. Even after you grow up, it's warm and familiar and delicious.

"Scrooge, the rich, avaricious man who doesn't trust anyone, sees his friend who died a long time ago on the night of Christmas Eve, and he's advised to change his ways. His friend gives Scrooge an opportunity and a wish. The three ghosts of Christmas past, present, and future appear to Scrooge one after another and show him things that he'd forgotten or chosen to overlook.

"A warm Christmas scene or a family going through life side by side despite their poverty or hope, trust; stuff like that.

"It's just like a meat loaf that mixes together celery, carrots, onions, whole eggs, and olives cooked up fragrant in an oven, slicing it up with a knife; then you cut it up with a fork and take little bites.

"The celery and carrots you usually hate intertwine gently, subtly with the meat juices, and a refreshing sense of happiness fills your heart. The slightly salty, unique aroma of the olives also feels delicious."

As she expounded with a beaming expression, she tore off a small corner of the page and brought it to her mouth.

Making a faint *kssh-kssh* sound, she swallowed, her white throat just barely moving, and then she smiled happily.

The clear sunlight streaming in the window gently colored her long, thin braids like cats' tails, her small white face, her thin limbs.

Standing rooted beside the table, I felt like I was in a dream.

She's . . . the real Tohko.

There could be no other bizarre high school girl who expounded on a book as she crumpled it up and ate it.

"What're you doing?" I asked, finally finding my voice.

Tohko slowly turned her face to me, and she smiled cutely.

"I was wondering how you were doing. I just came for a little breather."

"You've got a lot of time for someone getting Fs."

"With your snacks to eat, I'm working really hard, so I should have at least a C now," she answered lazily, totally unruffled by my jab.

But instead, I relaxed and snorted.

Tohko rested both her arms on the back of the chair and looked up at me with kind, peaceful eyes.

"Hey, Konoha. The snacks you've been putting in the mailbox this whole time have been really good. Crispy cookies baked with sesame, raisin cake with a slight taste of alcohol . . . peppermint jelly, sweet chai . . . I ate them up and imagined that even though I'm not around, you're having fun . . . that something good must have happened to you."

My heart fluttered at her clear voice, and I quickly looked away.

"I couldn't make a girl studying for her exams eat anything weird, could I? You're such a pig, you'd eat the whole thing."

"Too true. But it's something you wrote, Konoha. I would never leave any behind."

What a crock. Even if it wasn't me writing, she would eat every last scrap of whatever bizarre letters got stuffed into our mailbox.

"Actually, though, lately your snacks have been a little bitter, Konoha…"

Tohko's face clouded over.

Had she come to see me because she was worried about me, then? Had my improv stories been that bitter?

I felt myself beginning to weaken somehow, felt my throat growing hot, and was on the verge of dumping all of it on Tohko.

No. I didn't want to do something so childish. Not when Tohko was so busy with her exams.

As I gritted my teeth and forced the impulse down, Tohko suddenly grinned.

"Talking about snacks has given me a craving for something sweet." She pressed, rattling her metal chair. "So, Konoha, what are you dropping off for me today?"

"Oh, I know. I'll write something up right now."

After I said it, I realized that I'd thrown an improv story I'd written earlier into my bag. It was the "essence of a fluffy, therapeutic vanilla soufflé" that I'd struggled over and fiddled with endlessly and then held in reserve the day that Kotobuki told me she hated me.

I took it out of my bag and set it on the table.

Then I wrote my cell phone number and e-mail address in ballpoint pen on a sky-blue bookmark lying nearby.

Tohko watched me, her face expectant, urging me to "Hurry, hurryyy."

I held the paper in my right hand and the bookmark in my left, turned to Tohko, and asked, "Do you want the big one or the small one?"

Tohko reached out with both hands, her whole face beaming, without getting up from the seat.

"The big one!"

After Tohko had eaten the essence of a fluffy, therapeutic vanilla soufflé with "butterfly," "Mount Fear," and "a surfer," she clutched at her chest, wearing a tortured look.

"Uggggh. That macho surfer came sliding down Mount Fear in nothing but a *Speedo*! His soul turned into a butterfly and slipped out of his body, then went back to Mount Fearrr! The surfer turned into a *skel*eton! Is this a horror story? Is it? This isn't vanilla; it tastes like fish cake with pickled radishes in itttt! It's not airy at *all*. It's all pricklyyyy. Augh, there's even ground wasabi in heeeere!"

I turned my back on Tohko as she blubbered and slipped the bookmark into my student planner.

I didn't give it to her after all.

"Urgh...ack...Hey, Konoha, what were you and Ryuto talking about on the phone?"

When I turned around, Tohko was clinging to the back of her chair, desperately fighting back her nausea.

Even so, she whispered haltingly, "Is there something that's bothering you maybe? If you tell your president, maybe we'll come up with a good idea."

I couldn't answer right away. In a strained voice, I asked, "Did Ryuto say something?"

"No. I heard him saying your name in the other room."

"Were you eavesdropping?"

As soon as I took the jab at her, she jolted forward in the chair and started arguing heatedly.

"N-no! I didn't have a glass up to the wall or anything! I don't care how mean Ryuto was for not telling me, and even if I could hear everything through the paper-thin walls and even if I got worried because when Ryuto was talking to you on the phone it sounded pretty involved, I would never do something so crass as to eavesdrop!"

"There's a ring from the glass around your ear."

"What?!"

I pointed, and Tohko clapped a hand over her right ear.

"Not really."

"Urk."

"You did eavesdrop, didn't you?"

When I pressed her, she grew defiant this time and began throwing a tantrum.

"But, but, but—it sounded like you were asking Ryuto for advice, and I worried and I could hardly study then! If I don't find out, I'll fail my exams and have to spend a whole 'nother year studying. If that happens, it'll be your fault, Konoha! That's right. It's your fault for depending on Ryuto. So in order for your beloved president to be at ease and focus on her exams, come clean and admit what's going on."

Sigh... Tohko was still Tohko.

Her selfish diatribe had drained me of all my energy.

There was no way to avoid someone like her going off. Tohko was a thousand times more childish than me.

"Okay, I get it. You can stop rattling your chair around like that. You're going to fall over and hit your face again like you did before."

I sighed and sat at the table, then started telling her everything that had happened so far.

Tohko pulled her chair up to the table. She furrowed her brows and looked sad at the story I told, and partway through, she put her index finger lightly to her lips and sank into thought.

When I was done, Tohko murmured, "Konoha, tell me the hints Mito gave Nanase about her boyfriend in detail, please."

"Um...I'm pretty sure there were three of them. There are nine people in his family, he has a habit of walking around a desk when he's thinking, and he likes coffee, I think?"

"Hmm..."

Her index finger still resting on her lips, she lost herself in thought once more.

"That's unusual, having nine people in your family," I said.

"I think Mito's boyfriend might not have nine people in his family."

"Huh?"

"This hint could point to something else entirely."

"Something else? Like what?"

Tohko's brows knit, and she looked a little troubled.

"I'm sorry. I don't really know yet, either," she murmured apologetically. Then she said, "But maybe Camellia is taken from Dumas's *Camille*."

"*Camille*? Oh, that's an opera, right?"

Tohko started to tell me about *Camille*.

"Yes. The original title of *Camille* is *La Dame aux Camélias*—which is French for 'the lady of the camellias.' The author is Dumas *fils*, whose father is the popular author Alexandre Dumas, famous for writing *The Three Musketeers* and *The Count of Monte Cristo*. Generally, the father is called Dumas *père* and the son Dumas *fils*.

"During his youth, Dumas *fils* was madly in love with Marie Duplessis, a high-end courtesan who was the cherry of the Parisian social world. He wrote *Camille* with her as his model.

"The protagonist is the naive young man, Armand—he's a little like Raoul in *Phantom of the Opera* actually. When he comes to Paris, Armand falls in love with the courtesan Marguerite, who's called 'the lady of the camellias.' Armand runs headlong into an intense passion, and Marguerite does love him but suffers from a disease of the lungs. Armand's father convinces her to leave his son, so she tearfully steps aside. It tastes like a bonbon of high-grade whiskey inside expensive, bitter chocolate: sweet and glamorous, a little bitter, and melancholy."

Mito, who wanted to become an opera singer, would naturally have known about *Camille*.

And that the heroine Marguerite was a courtesan.

And if she had given herself the name "Camellia" because of that...what had been going through Mito's mind when she did that?

Tohko told me the rest of the story.

"In the opera by Verdi, he changed the names from Armand to Alfredo and from Marguerite to Violetta. The last scene is a little different, too, and the title is *La Traviata*. In Italian, that means 'a woman who's strayed from the path.'"

My face twisted as pain stabbed into my heart.

A woman who's strayed from the path.

Had Mito strayed from the path like the lady of the camellias had?

Had she wandered into a place from which she couldn't return as a result?

Or had she hidden herself away for someone else's benefit the way the lady of the camellias had withdrawn for Armand's sake?

Where was Mito's Raoul, her Armand? Or had he never existed like Kotobuki said?

With an intelligent look in her eyes, Tohko said, "Mito's story definitely resembles the *Phantom of the Opera*. The real-life operas *Faust* and *Don Juan* appear in the *Phantom of the Opera*, too.

"But if we're assuming that this disappearance is like the one in the *Phantom of the Opera*, then there's a major hint you guys missed."

"What do you mean?"

I placed my hands on the table and leaned forward.

"Why hasn't Mito been dropped from the lead in the recital? If she's missed ten days of rehearsals without permission, that's strange. I know people are saying that she's taking special lessons in secret or that she's got a powerful backer, but I think there has to be pressure coming from somewhere.

"That person must be confident that she'll appear in the actual show, right? In *Phantom of the Opera*, the Phantom threatens the opera's owner and puts his beloved Christine onstage as the stand-in for the diva Carlotta. In order to do that, the Phantom changes Carlotta's voice to that of a toad, and he even sabotages a performance."

"Are you saying Mito's supporter is the Phantom—her angel?"

Tohko nodded, her face serious.

"There is that possibility. There's a limited number of people in a position to interfere with the casting. A teacher at the school, someone in the administration...whoever it is, that person might know Mito's whereabouts."

My breath caught.

"Well, Konoha?" Tohko asked. "Are you going to look into it?"

Every other time, she had said, "This is a top-priority investigation, Konoha!" and flown off without the least concern for my situation.

Pursing her lips, her gaze bright, she waited for my reply with great patience, like an older sister watching over the disappointment of a younger brother.

Her eyes said, "You decide, Konoha."

My heart swelled, and my insecurity and hesitation rose up in my throat, competing with my desire to push ahead.

What more could I possibly do? I hadn't even told Kotobuki yet that Mito might have been an escort.

But…

With Tohko watching me like this, I no longer wanted to turn my back on this. If I did, things would be the same as they had always been.

I got my breathing under control and answered, "Yes."

Instantly, Tohko's face broke into a smile.

Her lips curved upward sweetly, gently, as if light were melting out of her.

She popped her index finger against my forehead; then in a bright voice. Tohko said, "Oookay! This is a top-priority investigation, Konoha."

"Please go home, Tohko."

"Whaaa—? *Why?*"

I was heading to the music hall on campus; behind me, Tohko shook her head petulantly and chased after me.

"You're going to see Maki, right? Then it's definitely better if I go with you."

"I can't let someone studying for their exams pose nude and catch a cold. Please go home and study."

"So you're going to get naked, then? You're going to pose nude?"

"That's not what I—"

"I can't let my precious snack writer—I mean, my underclassman—fall into Maki's grasp."

"But, Tohko, didn't you send me as a messenger before because you didn't want to see Maki yourself?"

"I just so happened to have an engagement I couldn't get out of that day."

While still butting heads, we ended up reaching the hall in the central yard.

In her personal workroom on the top floor of the music hall,

Maki Himekura, aka the Princess, heard us out with a bemused smile.

"And which of you is going to strip for me? Tohko? Or perhaps Konoha?"

She was wearing a work apron over her school uniform and held a paintbrush in one hand.

Her long brown hair was wavy and encircled her face like a mane, then flowed down her back. Maki, who was also tall and voluptuous with glamorous features befitting the name Princess, was the granddaughter of the school's director. She knew everything and could get ahold of anything.

However, for any information she gave out, she always required compensation.

And Maki's premier desire was to draw a nude portrait of Tohko. Apparently she'd been trying to convince Tohko to do it for three years now. Because of that, Tohko was completely on guard against her.

Although since Maki was the type of person who said stuff like "It gives me a thrill when Tohko hates me," she was probably A-OK even if Tohko just glared at her or avoided her.

"This time, Tohko's not involved. I'll pay the compensation."

"No. As your president and as a book girl, I can't stand silently by and watch in my underclassman's gravest hour."

"Being a book girl has nothing to do with anything, though."

"Underclassmen are supposed to make their seniors look good."

"Oh, so you're stripping for me then, Tohko?"

"What?!"

As soon as Maki turned her smarmy smile on her, Tohko began to stutter.

"W-we're going to...negotiate that later. And, uh, I've been eating too many snacks lately and put on weight...If I was to do

102

something like that, I'd need some time to get ready. And hey, aren't you busy studying for exams, too, Maki?! You don't have time to be painting."

"Hmm? I've already gotten a recommendation to a school."

"B…but, I'm getting Fs, s-so I have to study…So, uh, I mean…p-put it on my tab!"

Watching Tohko ball up her fists and yell mightily, Maki burst out laughing, unable to hold back any longer.

"Oh geez, you're *so* cute! How can you stand it? All right. I'm drawing a different model right now anyway, so I'll put it on your tab. You're going to pay me back tenfold before we graduate."

"Urk!"

Tohko was speechless. Maki gazed at her with a suspicious glint in her eyes.

"This will be my early Christmas present to you. Oh, oh! Don't forget my present has *interest*."

Even as I felt the deepest sympathy for Tohko, in my heart I secretly whispered, *That's why you shouldn't have come. There's no way you were going to be a match for Maki, and now you got what you deserved…*

The Princess worked fast.

Saturday night, Tohko and I were in a hotel room.

Tohko had let down her braids and tied her hair back casually below her ears with a pink rubber band, rolled up the waist of her uniform skirt to make it shorter, and she bubbled with excitement.

I was wearing street clothes, a knit shirt and jeans, and had my hand pressed to my head with a distressed visage.

"Wow, this dinette set is so pretty! I think it's an antique! And the springs in this bed are so bouncy! Look, look!"

Tohko knelt on the luxurious double bed and bounced it up

and down to show me. This was the first time in my life I'd been alone in a hotel room with a girl. And for it to be with Tohko!

As she bounced on the bed, Tohko lost her balance and tumbled off.

"Geez, Tohko, please just go home."

"No way. This *ploy* isn't going to work without me," she declared after fixing her skirt and standing back up.

This ploy... you decided to do this all on your own, Tohko...

"Are you really going to do it?"

"Yup."

"You should be parked at your desk studying for your exams."

"I did a bunch of math problems last night, so it's fine."

I picked that apart. "Why are you still doing math problems?"

"Because I need it for the National Center Test obviously."

"The National Center Test? You don't mean you're taking exams for the national schools! Are you doing it for souvenirs?" I asked her, so shocked that I forgot where we were and what we were doing.

I was sure she would try for the literature department of a private school, but the national schools! With those disastrous math scores, how could she even think about taking national school exams?! She was way out of her league!

Tohko puffed out her perfectly flat chest proudly.

"Heh-heh. I'm gonna sweep the national schools."

"Cut it out. You're just throwing the exam fees away. And *sweep* them?! You're being way too reckless! You have to switch your sights to a private school right away."

Geez, and with Fs? No wonder I'd thought it was weird. But she would have been able to get such decent marks in literature...

I was utterly appalled. Hunkered on the bed, Tohko pouted and leaned forward to glower at me.

"You're *AW-ful!* You're sooo not considerate enough to someone studying to get into college!"

"But, Tohko, you need to understand your own limits. Let's just go home."

"No. I changed clothes and everything."

"All you did was take down your braids."

"I made my skirt three inches shorter, too. That's a big deal for a girl."

"This kind of ploy is totally pointless. How are we going to ask about Mito by pretending to be an escort?"

"It's fine. I'm a book girl who's read *Lady Chatterley's Lover* by Lawrence, and *Hell in the Bottle* by Kyusaku Yumeno, and the Sleeping Beauty trilogy by Rice, including *The Claiming of Sleeping Beauty*, *Beauty's Punishment*, and *Beauty's Release* cover to cover. Even if I don't have any experience, I've got the knowledge covered."

"You can't learn from those! Or actually, just *don't* learn from them!"

While we were arguing, we heard the sound of the door opening.

"Konoha, hide!"

Tohko pushed me away, and I hurried to conceal myself behind the curtain.

The very next second, a man in his midforties wearing a suit came into the room, toying with his mustache.

There was no mistaking him. I'd seen him in a photo. It was Kengo Tsutsumi, the assistant director of Shirafuji Music Academy.

Tsutsumi was a regular on the members-only underage escort site that Camellia was on, and he was one of Camellia's "customers." He was also the person who had leveraged Mito into the lead role of the recital.

He didn't look like anything more than an ordinary, greasy, middle-aged man, but could he be Mito's angel?

Tohko turned around on the bed and hung her head.

"I kept you waiting, didn't I?"

Tsutsumi sat down on the edge of the bed, too, and peeked up at Tohko's face indecently.

"Are you nervous? Don't tell me this is this your first time?"

Tohko answered, her voice soft, "I heard...you can make a lot of money..."

"That's true. If I like you, I'll give you money, and I'll buy you anything you want."

Twitch...Tohko's shoulders moved.

"Really? Anything?"

"Yeah. What do you want?"

The next instant, Tohko suddenly threw her whole body against Tsutsumi and began talking, her eyes glinting like stars.

"I'd love to eat the first editions of Ogai Mori's collected works all at once! And then there's Sōseki Natsume and Junichiro Tanizaki, and Saisei Muro, and ohhh, it'd be tough to leave out a first edition of Ichiyō Higuchi's *Growing Up*! Also the works of Chekhov that have gone out of print and, ooooh, it's been a dream of mine to get together the whole back catalog of Harlequin Historicals, pile them up in my room, and then devour every one! I thought that if I won the lottery, I'd be able to make it come true for sure!

"It would feel exactly like a huge cream puff stuffed with custard that has a little rum in it, and the dense flavor of a Sacher torte, and drowning in an ocean of fragrant champagne jelly!"

Partway through, the force of her enthusiasm had pushed Tsutsumi over, but Tohko kept on talking despite that, and Tsutsumi looked up at her, his eyes panicked.

Though I could feel a headache coming, I jumped out, pointed my cell phone at Tsutsumi, and took a picture.

"Who are you?!"

I showed the picture I'd just taken to Tsutsumi as he hurriedly crawled out from under Tohko and coldly told him, "Mr. Kengo Tsutsumi, if you don't want me to send this image to the director of Shirafuji Music Academy, who happens to be your father-in-law, or to your other coworkers, will you tell me about the girl you called Camellia?"

"C-Camellia...?!"

Tsutsumi appeared to take a terrible shock; he paled and fell silent.

What Tsutsumi told us then, his body shaking feebly, was as follows.

Right after Yuka Mito disappeared, he was sent an invitation to the recital in a red envelope with the name Camellia on it.

Typed out in computer characters was a message that Yuka Mito was taking lessons at a certain location and that since she would perform at the recital without fail, she was not to be dropped from the lead. If that was to happen, his honor might risk losing his current position.

"Yuka was so quiet and amateurish, and I was quite fond of her. But despite that, she suddenly started threatening me, saying that if I didn't make her the lead for the recital, she would reveal what she'd done with me.

"That day, Yuka tapped my cheek with a butcher's knife and told me: 'You could let me watch you cut your wrists and commit suicide right here, too. That would be quite a scandal.' She looked at me and talked like she wasn't all there. Or so I thought when she suddenly burst out crying or grappling like a wild animal or glowering into space with empty eyes. Anyway, she was a wreck.

"I was relieved when she disappeared, but then she started sending me letters and e-mails. She was an unbelievable slut! That girl is a demon wearing the mask of an angel! I'm a victim!"

We watched Tsutsumi vent his hatred of Yuka, thinking unbearable thoughts.

Camellia was Yuka Mito.

And what's more, Mito had blackmailed Tsutsumi in order to play the lead role at the recital, and she was still manipulating him from the shadows.

As we walked along a cool, dark road that night, the air seeming to freeze around us, Tohko and I tended toward silence. Tohko's skirt had returned to its usual length, but we couldn't erase what we'd heard from our minds.

Bitter thoughts spread through my heart. The Yuka Mito that we'd heard about from Tsutsumi was a far cry from the dear friend that Kotobuki had talked about.

I could never tell Kotobuki that the Phantom's true identity was Christine herself.

What in the world was Mito trying to accomplish?

Christine's heart was inscrutable to me.

In front of a gorgeously constructed stage set, Christine tells Raoul, "Look, Raoul, at these walls, this forest, this tunnel of trees, this painted canvas image. They've all witnessed a sublime passion like no other. So people with far more poetic spirits than most have produced these pictures in this place.

"Our love is perfect for this place, don't you think, Raoul? After all, our love is a fabrication, too, and oh! Nothing more than an illusion!"

⟶◆⟵

These words that sounded so innocent cut into Raoul's—into my—heart.

Perhaps the love, the hope, the dreams, everything that I had once believed in had been nothing more than illusions.

I wonder if Kotobuki was at this moment still worrying about her best friend, if she was praying that Mito would come home safe and they'd be able to go back to their quiet lives, exactly as they had been before.

The air prickled at my skin. Tohko would look over at me in concern every now and again.

As we were parting ways, Tohko suddenly said, "Hey, Konoha. Did you finish reading *Phantom of the Opera*?"

"Nope."

My listless answer got me this from Tohko: "Oh...you should try reading it to the end. The story overlaps with Mito's so it might be tough to read, but...even so, I think the truth of the story is at the end."

She spoke quietly, then watched me with a slightly worried look again.

I hated myself for making her look like that, and deep in my chest I felt a fiery pain, as if it was being scraped.

"Tohko..."

"Hmm?"

"Please...study hard."

I acted tough, pretending not to be hurt, and Tohko gave me a faint smile.

"I will."

With a cowardly look, I watched Tohko, her loose hair swaying evanescently, as she disappeared into her neighborhood.

Left on my own, I continued walking, so tired that it felt as if I'd aged considerably. I closed down my heart and tried not to think about anything.

How much time passed while I did that? I wondered.

Suddenly my cell phone vibrated in my coat pocket.

When I pulled it out and checked, it was an unknown number.

I recalled the message I'd been sent before and my body tensed a little. I pressed the talk button and put it to my ear.

"Inoue?"

A girl's voice I didn't recognize spoke my name.

A majestic, pretty voice that carried well.

Who was this? It seemed that she knew me.

"Nice to meet you, I suppose. I'm Yuka Mito."

A cold gust of wind blew into my face.

It was Yuka Mito!

My heart was raging almost painfully, and my brain was burning. I told myself I had to calm down and tightened my grip on the phone with my sweating hand. Earnestly I asked, "You're Kotobuki's friend, Mito?"

"That's right."

"How do you know about me?"

"I know lots about you, Inoue. Nanase is always talking about you. Nothing but you for a long, long time on the phone or in e-mails."

She didn't seem to be mocking me; her tone was more placid and kind. In the same instant that the sound of her voice pierced my heart, I felt confused.

"What about my phone number? How'd you get that?"

"That's a secret. But once I decide to get ahold of something, most things wind up mine. Besides people's hearts, of course."

"That's creepy."

"I'm sorry."

Mito apologized offhandedly. She was so calm; she didn't seem like someone who was missing. Tsutsumi's voice, declaring *"Yuka is a demon,"* echoed in my ears.

"Are you the one who sent me that text before, too? The one that said, 'He's Lucifer'?"

"That's right."

"Why would you do something like that? Who is it?"

"He's right beside you two. The fallen angel who was cast into Hell for the sin of pride and who became Satan. You shouldn't get close to him."

"I don't understand what you're saying."

"I'm saying, don't do anything stupid."

Her voice turned suddenly frigid.

"You saw Tsutsumi today, right? That's a problem."

My skin prickled with terror. She knew that we'd met Tsutsumi in that hotel? Had she been watching? Where from? Or had Tsutsumi told her?

I listened as hard as I could and tried to discern the sounds of where she was.

The sound of a car's engine.

The faint honking of a horn.

The melody of "Jingle Bells" playing…

"Don't interfere with me. And don't get Nanase involved, either."

"If you came back, Kotobuki and I wouldn't be looking for you. Where are you?!"

"I'm inside a Christmas tree. That's my home."

"Jingle Bells" shifted into the refrain. The voices sang brightly, joyfully of Christmas cheer.

"…I saw your profile on that website."

"It's nothing special."

"Even the part where you said Miu Inoue was your favorite author?"

"That's the truth."

"Kotobuki didn't tell me you were a fan of Miu Inoue."

"That's because Nanase seems to hate her for some reason. I love her. Miu Inoue...I've read her so many times I practically memorized it...But that doesn't matter anymore," Mito said coolly.

"Kotobuki's worried about you. She's waiting for you to come home. You made a promise to her, didn't you? You said that you'd keep Christmas open for her."

Her pretty voice, as clear as water, was tinged with a trace of sadness.

"Yes. I did make a promise...to Nanase...and to my boyfriend. That I would spend Christmas Eve with him and Christmas with her."

"Then it's not just Kotobuki who's waiting for you. He must be, too."

"No!"

Her voice grew the harshest it had been so far and became emotional. The sound of a car passing drowned out the Christmas songs.

"Christine is with the angel. She can't see Raoul ever again. She's already taken her ring off."

Without understanding what those words meant, I shouted at her, only wanting to bring her back.

"Your angel's true identity is the Phantom, though! You can't stay with a guy like that!"

What I heard next was a frigid voice, like ice stabbing into my chest.

"You're the same as Raoul. You fear what you don't understand and try to shut it away. What on earth can that idiot Raoul do? Christine passed away listening to a hymn."

"I haven't understood a single thing you've said."

"There's nothing left to talk about. Just don't get Nanase in-volved. She's the only thing you need to keep your eyes on, Inoue."

"Wait! Don't hang up!"

There was a click, and my voice broke off. The warmth drained out of my body rapidly, and shaking with the cold that crawled up my legs, I played Mito's words over again in my head.

"Christine passed away listening to a hymn."

Was Mito Christine? What did it mean that she'd passed away listening to a hymn?!

———◆———

This is a catastrophe! Raoul wasn't in time.

The angel cut my hand off! I was obstinate and wouldn't let go of the ring. I clung to it, so the angel flew into a rage like a pitch-black flame, and he sawed my left hand off, then carved off each of my fingers.

Warm blood dripped down my wrist like water, dyeing the earth, and a rank, awful smell filled the area. Then the angel picked up the blood-spattered ring and with his cold tongue licked off the blood that clung to it.

That was a ritual to link the angel and I deeply together.

I can never go back, neither to Nanase nor to my boyfriend. Dragged into the shadows of this night, imprisoned, I've become a phantom who cannot be allowed to bare her face and walk in the sunlight.

The angel destroyed me! He seduced me with a pure voice, spoke kind words, and stroked my hair to lower my guard, to make me trust him, to trick me! He sullied my body, my voice, my heart; remade me as a terrifying monster; turned me into his companion!

The angel was a disfigured phantom wearing a mask!

Why did I do such a thing as believe a terrifying abomination with that sullied name? Why did I open my heart to him, going to see him each night, mingling our voices beneath the moon and singing?

That was a cowardly trap!

The Phantom cut my wrist and stole the precious ring that was the proof of my love for my boyfriend. And he separated me from my normal life.

If I hadn't met the Phantom, I might have been able to go back to the warm, gentle place where Nanase and my boyfriend were.

I might have been able to start over as a normal girl there.

What I got in exchange for my false prosperity was only a fearful destruction, a cold mask, and a pitch-dark castle like a mausoleum that the Phantom made.

Christine passed away!

Christine passed away!

Christine passed away!

The final hymn melted away like dew into the shadows. In my despair, I heard the sound of my heart come to a stop.

There is nothing left here now but the Phantom who crawls pathetically through the grass and who, with glinting eyes, grants revenge against the people of the daylight world.

How sad would Nanase be if she found out about this? How much would it hurt her? When I look at my phone, I've got a message from Nanase and a voice mail. She's probably waiting for a reply and worrying.

I have to send Nanase a message. She's the only one I want to protect. I need Nanase to be smiling.

But what's this?! Christine's skeleton is in the depths of the earth, and I've been transformed into a corrupted phantom—

⟫⦿⟪

At the start of the week, during a break on Monday, I went to the teacher's office and found out that Mr. Mariya had quit the school. I was left gaping.

"No way! But the second term's not over yet! How come?!"

The teacher who told me about it frowned and answered, "I heard that there was some tragedy in his family, but I don't really know," and he reminded me not to tell the other students yet.

A leaden anxiety sank into the depths of my heart.

While thinking over what Mito had said to me on the phone that weekend, I recalled the musician who had slashed his wrists while listening to hymns, which Mr. Mariya had told me about.

I was starting to wonder if there was a connection to Mito saying that Christine had passed away listening to a hymn and had intended to ask Mr. Mariya for more details, but now he had left the school!

Unable to accept this news, I went to Maki's class during lunch. But Maki hadn't been there all that morning, either.

What now…?

At a loss, I walked toward the music room. Because that was just about the only place I could think of that had a connection to Mr. Mariya.

Mr. Mariya had disappeared, too, not just Mito. The last time we'd talked, Mr. Mariya had raised his paper cup of cold chai in one hand and said with a faint smile.

"You know, Inoue, success is a fleeting thing for an artist. Personally, I choose to have this cup of chai instead."

I couldn't believe Mr. Mariya, who had loved the peace of every-day life more than anything, would throw it all away so easily. Not Mr. Mariya who had told me that he was here now so that he could like himself...

In the short time Kotobuki, Mr. Mariya, and I had spent to-gether, he had given me important advice.

And when I'd told him I was going to help her, he had smiled and said, "I'll be here." But now he'd suddenly disappeared with-out a word to us. It was a huge shock. I felt as if a giant chasm was yawning open in my chest.

I got to the door of the music room and was just about to put my hand on the doorknob when I abruptly stopped and perked up my ears.

I heard a low voice inside.

Peeking in from a crack in the door, I saw a girl in a school uni-form crumpled up on the floor, crying.

In front of her I saw finely shredded pieces of red paper scat-tered around. I gasped and pushed the door wide open.

She jumped in surprise and looked up at me, her eyes wet with tears, a petite girl with childlike features.

I had seen her somewhere before.

Of course! It was the girl who'd been in here kissing Mr. Mariya before!

"Did you hear about Mr. Mariya quitting, too?" I asked. The girl nodded, and tears started pouring down her face again.

I walked over to stand in front of the girl and comforted her, saying, "Don't worry," waiting for her to calm down.

Her name was Sugino, and she was a first-year. She hadn't been dating Mr. Mariya; rather, it had been unrequited love.

As I listened to her story, my eyes ran casually over the red paper scattered everywhere. Just as I'd suspected, it had been an envelope.

"A red envelope with a ticket to the recital inside came from the name Camellia..."

I remembered Tsutsumi's story and felt a chill.

"Did you tear this up? How come?"

"*Snff*...'Cos ever since that letter came, Marmar's been acting weird...He started organizing these files all of a sudden, and even though I offered to help, he told me I couldn't. He always treated me like a kid and not like an equal, but then out of nowhere, he invited me to a hotel...But even then, he just left without doing anything."

She said Mr. Mariya had acted strangely even after they went into the hotel. He walked cautiously around the room, as if he was looking for something, and then when Sugino had showered and come back, he was fixated on the bedside table with a grim expression she had never seen before, and he'd been whispering.

"What was he saying?"

"I...I couldn't really hear him, but... 'I'm too late' and 'The angel took her...'"

The angel!

"Then he just walked out of the room."

The kiss I'd witnessed in the music room had happened the next day. Apparently it had been his apology to Sugino, who had been indignant at being abandoned in the hotel.

Just hearing about how Mr. Mariya had acted, it sounded unnatural. And then he'd said, "angel."

"Since Marmar always looked really pained when he was looking at the envelope, I started wondering what was inside it...I snuck it out of Marmar's desk. But there was only an opera ticket in it—no letter."

After that, she revealed in a quiet voice, she'd been unable to find the right moment to return it, and she'd held on to the envelope all that time.

"Did you see who sent it?"

"Yeah. It said Camellia."

A shock ran through my skull.

It was identical to the envelope Tsutsumi had gotten. What did this mean?!

Did Mr. Mariya know Camellia?! Was he involved in Mito's disappearance?!

Anxiety threatened to send me reeling, and my breathing grew labored. But Mr. Mariya had said he wasn't that close to Mito...

Sugino kept crying, but I managed to calm her down and returned to class right before lunch ended.

I nearly collided with Kotobuki at the door.

We were both surprised and backed up.

"...S-sorry!"

"N-no problem."

Kotobuki bit down on her lip and looked at me meekly. It looked like there was something she wanted to say.

I looked back at her as I struggled over whether or not I should tell her that I'd gotten a call from Mito or about Mr. Mariya.

At that moment, a shrill ring emanated from Kotobuki's skirt.

Kotobuki went completely white and pulled her phone out of her pocket to look at it, spinning so her back was toward me and then rushing off. Who in the world could be calling her? What was it about?

I was bursting with a desire to run after her and ask. But the teacher was coming, so I went back to my seat.

Kotobuki was staring at her cell phone, hidden under her desk, with a tense expression.

<hr />

When classes were over, Mori and the others surrounded Kotobuki, and they left together. They were going to a crepe shop apparently. Kotobuki's friends were probably worried about her because she was so down.

Akutagawa went to his team practice, and I left the room feeling antsy.

I could feel the normalcy that surrounded us fracturing and threatening to break apart so intensely that it pressed down on my chest, and I had no idea how to react to it.

Why had Mr. Mariya invited Sugino to a hotel? Why had he acted the way he did?

I had no leads left besides Omi. He apparently hated Mr. Mariya, and he'd warned me not to get close to him. Maybe he would know about this teacher that Kotobuki and I didn't recognize. And about the angel, and Mito...

I was afraid to talk to him even now and didn't know if he would give me a complete answer even if I did ask, but there was nothing I could do but throw myself into it. I would just go to the library, and if he wasn't there, I would ask one of the staff where his homeroom was...

Just then, in the hall that led to the library, I saw a boy wearing glasses standing at the window, and I quailed.

Omi—

The instant I felt his frigid gaze turn on me, I felt as if claws were digging into my heart and I flinched.

Omi muttered in a low, threatening voice, "Stop lurking. You're going to get hurt. *And not just you. Nanase Kotobuki will, too.*"

As soon as I heard that, heat flared at my temples.

"What are you going to do to Kotobuki?! You're not sending her any weird messages, are you?"

He gave me a thin smile.

"And if I were?"

Something burst inside my head, and I grabbed hold of him.

It was an act I never would have imagined myself capable of, but it wasn't simply because I remembered how pale Kotobuki's face had been as she looked at the message; I was probably also driving back my terror, which was a trembling I could feel in my core.

I gripped his collar in both hands and shook him, shouting, "What did you do to Kotobuki?! What do you know?!" Omi clucked his tongue, and the confrontation turned into a minor scuffle.

Just then a silver chain spilled out from beneath his collar.

At the end of it, I saw a thin silver ring, and a shudder ran up my spine.

"She's already taken her ring off."

The ring glinting on his chest was an accessory anyone could buy in a shop. It wasn't so strange for a high school boy to wear jewelry nowadays.

But not something like that...

Omi grabbed the ring that had fallen out in one hand and fixed his glinting eyes on me in a glare.

"Stop howling. There's nothing you can do anyway. You're just like that idiot Raoul."

Then as I stood rooted and gaping, he said in a cold voice filled with hatred, *"Aren't you, Miu?"*

A shock pierced my heart, and I felt as if the familiar sights around me were warping crazily in that moment.

Confusion and terror assaulted me like black waves, as if I had been shut up in a different dimension that someone else controlled.

How did he know about Miu?!

And how did he know that I was Miu Inoue?!

There was no way he could have. But he'd definitely said it just now!

That accursed name that I'd kept hidden, the name of Miu Inoue—!

He'd said it to me!

The boy who stood before me seemed an unsettling, enigmatic creature, and a chill coursed through my body. My legs were trembling.

In my confusion and fear, he loosed his final blow on me with a cold stare.

"You've never held anything heavier than a pen, have you, *Miu*?"

I took a staggering step back, then turned my back on him and started running.

"Stop lurking. You're going to get hurt."

"And not just you. Nanase Kotobuki will, too."

"Aren't you, Miu?"

His words—his voice—echoed in my mind.

"Miu, Miu, Miu, Miu, Miu—"

Quick, quick—I had to get somewhere his voice wouldn't reach me.

I'd been bitten by an angel with his fangs bared!

Even when I got home and closed the door to my room, I couldn't get my shock under control.

My mind was in turmoil, and I couldn't get it organized. Why had Omi said that to me? I'd never even told my friends in middle school that I was Miu Inoue. I was sure that the only people who knew Miu Inoue's true identity were my family, my publisher, and Miu.

Even now it seemed that I could hear his voice. I put my headphones on in a daze, started some music, and turned up the volume. I lay in bed like that, cradling my head in my arms and closing my eyes.

What *was* he? Did that ring belong to Mito?

Was Mito with him? What about Mr. Mariya—Kotobuki—?

I desperately thought about other things, trying to forget the name Miu; about what had happened; about the *Phantom of the Opera*, which I'd been reading at night—but my thoughts tumbled back to the same place again and again and kept replaying the same scene.

Raoul and the Persian were cruelly cornered by the Phantom, who had cast off his angel's mask.

The Phantom flaunted his power for Christine and laid bare his crazed obsession with her, forcing her to love him.

"I have invented a mask that makes me look like anybody. People will not even turn around in the streets. You will be the happiest of women. And we will sing, all by ourselves, till we swoon away with delight!"

"You are crying! You are afraid of me!"

"I am not really wicked! Love me and you shall see!"

"If you loved me I should be as gentle as a lamb!"

"You don't love me! You don't love me! You don't love me!"

Knowing that Christine's heart didn't belong to him, the Phantom's anger turned on Raoul, his rival for her love. Christine tries to protect Raoul. But inside the vast subterranean labyrinth the Phantom constructed, he has Raoul at his mercy and hunts him down. The Phantom was so terribly powerful and overwhelming that fighting back was futile.

"There's nothing you can do anyway. You're just like that idiot Raoul."

The cold voice filled with contempt crept into my mind, accompanied by the giggling of a young girl.

*"I will remove you from **his** power, Christine, I swear it! And you shall not think of him anymore."*

He could never have toppled the Phantom with only integrity and passion.

And besides, did Christine want to be saved? If Christine had actually chosen to reign in that subterranean kingdom with the Phantom, then Raoul was beyond help.

I'd become Raoul without noticing it.

A chuckling voice pursued me as I ran around in the darkness underground.

"Don't come for me. Go away! Don't make me listen to that voice!"

Ahead, a faint light appeared. I had to get to it!

But when I reached my destination, frenzied, the Phantom stood there, his body obscured in a long black cloak, and his face covered with a white mask.

All of a sudden, the laughter stopped.

Within the frigid silence that enfolded the darkness, in the face of my terror, the Phantom slowly removed his mask.

Behind it appeared a girl I knew very well.

Miu!

A screaming cacophony rolled through the room, and the shadows fractured and fell away.

"*So you were the Phantom!*" I shouted in a voice that seemed ripped from my body.

Miu pointed at me, and her cold eyes declared:

"*No, the Phantom was you, Konoha.*"

I awoke to the vibrating of my cell phone against my cheek.

My whole body was drenched in sweat, and my bangs clung to my forehead. I answered without checking who it was, and a harried voice leaped to life in my ear.

"Inoue! It went to voice mail twice!"

"Mori...? Sorry, I didn't hear it. I was asleep. Did something happen?"

Mori cried in a rapid-fire voice, "Nanase's gone! Her mom called me. She said Nanase left home without a word and when she calls her cell phone, Nanase doesn't answer!"

◆

Oh, I hope Raoul doesn't come!

If he comes, the Phantom will kill him!

Please, don't lay a hand on Raoul. Don't hurt him.

Raoul isn't like us. He's a kind, innocent person who belongs under the sun. He's adorable, and good, and he laughs to hide his sadness—a melancholy, dear person that I care for, an important person. I love him!

I know it's an impossibility that he and I could stay together for the rest of our lives, like making a blue rose.

A blue rose is a false rose—a white rose that's been dyed—and real blue roses don't look purely blue.

Blue roses mean "something impossible," and our love is a thing like the fabricated blue rose. But even if it *is* an illusion, I love Raoul.

Please, don't come. Don't come, Raoul. I don't want to see you snared in the trap the Phantom has prepared for you, dragged into the darkness and painted in blood.

Don't come. Don't come, Raoul.

Don't come!!!

I've got messages and voice mail from Nanase.

The Christmas song I have as my ring tone played a ton of times.

Nanase was totally bewildered, and she was crying. She said she missed me. She asked me to come back. Said she didn't know what to do, that she would do anything, but she needed me, so please come back. Come back, come back, come back.

Out of everyone in the world, Nanase is the only one I didn't want to hurt. I wanted her to smile with joy. I'm defiled, and my love is defiled. My dream is defiled. My name is defiled.

But when I think of Nanase, I feel like my heart gets purified. All I hope for now is Nanase's happiness.

But Nanase is crying, and I can't comfort her. My dear, dear Nanase is crying, and I can't hug her. I can't even touch her or talk to her. Even though she's crying. Even though she's so afraid, so terrified, so hurt, so alone, and crying.

My heart is going to rip apart.

Chapter 5—That Was My First Love

Panting, I moved single-mindedly down the night-bound street, illuminated by a bright moon.

Besides the two messages from Mori, I had a message from Kotobuki in my voice mail, too.

In a frail voice, as if seeking help, she had said, "Inoue—! Yuka's grandma called me. She got the letter I sent her... Yuka's family's car fell into a lake over a month ago, and her whole family was in it. Her dad, her mom, and her little brother are all dead... They found a note, and it was a suicide... Inoue... Inoue, what should I do...?"

Why couldn't I have picked up the phone at such a critical moment?

The thought of how Kotobuki must have felt when she found out what happened to Mito's family made it impossible to forgive myself.

Mori had said that Kotobuki hadn't gone to the houses of any friends from school.

In which case, she might be there.

It was after midnight when I finally reached Mito's house.

Perhaps because the lights in the nearby houses were almost all out, the one building that had fallen into ruin felt even creepier than when we'd come before.

I went through the gate, which creaked as it swung on its hinges, and watching my step carefully, I approached the front door.

When I did, I noticed that faint light spilled from a window facing the yard.

I circled around that way, and when I peeked in through the broken glass, I saw Kotobuki wearing a coat, hunkered down in a corner of the room, curled up with her face buried in her knees.

All around her, candles shaped like stars, angels, and Christmas trees were arrayed as if on a birthday cake, shining faintly in the dark room.

I tapped softly on the window so as not to startle her.

"Kotobuki?"

She sluggishly lifted her head.

I saw her murmur "Inoue...," knitting her brow, her eyes full of tears. I felt a little relieved.

"I'm glad I found you. How did you get in there?"

"The window...I stuck my hand through the hole in the glass and unlocked the door..."

"Oh. Your mom's worried 'cos you disappeared without saying a word. Mori and the others, too."

Kotobuki looked sad and lowered her eyes timidly, but she circled her arms more tightly around her knees and didn't make a move to stand up. Maybe she still didn't have her emotions under control. It was only natural after hearing news like that...

I opened the glass window and went in without taking my shoes off. Kotobuki hesitantly raised her eyes to look at me.

"I'll sit down next to you."

She didn't say anything, so without waiting for a response, I sat down on the dust-caked wooden floor.

Kotobuki's face drooped a little again, and she curled up, resting her face on her knees.

The room was totally empty—there was no furniture, and it was chilly and smelled like smoke and mold.

The tiny flames burning around us flickered with slivers of orange light.

"Where did these candles come from?"

"I was going to give them to Yuka...for Christmas...I collected them, one or two at a time. Yuka loved Christmas trees and lights..."

My chest tightened at the frailty in her voice.

Christmas Eve with her boyfriend, Christmas with Nanase. That should have been a promise that she could keep...

"Y'know, Yuka would always say...how she wished she could live inside a Christmas tree. That it would probably be all glittery and beautiful...that it would probably feel like you were throwing a party every day..."

Her voice choked off, and Kotobuki buried her face in her knees again.

My chest felt tighter than ever.

When I'd asked Mito where she was during that phone call, I remembered that she had answered in a singsong tone, *"I'm inside a Christmas tree. That's my home."*

A glittering, dreamlike world unlike the everyday.

Had Mito longed for a fantastical place like that?

Had she wanted to go there?

Kotobuki's shoulders shook, and she let out a sob.

"Yuka's family...I can't believe they're...I wonder if Yuka knew about it...She has nowhere else to go...It's just too awful. I feel so bad for her. I wonder if the reason she disappeared was because she knew she was all alone."

That might be true, I thought with a creaking ache.

Mito, who had pretended on the surface to be cheerful and pursued her dreams of being a professional opera singer pure heartedly while earning money for school by working as an escort, might have been catapulted completely out of her ordinary life by the deaths of her family.

Having lost any place to call home and despairing, Mito would have nothing left to her but the illusory kingdom the Phantom had created. She would have no choice but to live there.

And maybe that was why she'd threatened Tsutsumi and gotten the lead role.

Her dream of succeeding as a diva may have been the only thing holding Mito up.

Tsutsumi had said as much, too. That Mito would start crying without warning or stare off into space with vacant eyes, and that she was a total wreck...She probably couldn't keep her mind balanced when such awful things kept happening.

Kotobuki buried her face in her knees and kept crying.

"...*Hic*...I wonder where Yuka is...I wonder what she's thinking."

Kotobuki couldn't be strong anymore; she could only curl up into a little ball and cry. Of course, I felt sorry for her and wanted to comfort her somehow, but I couldn't think of a good way to do it. My throat tightened, and my chest felt like it was ripping open.

"*Hk*...Yuka's pretty and...she's cheerful, and she had such amazing dreams, and she was working hard to make them come true, and I always used to brag about her. I would get excited thinking how Yuka was about to be a famous opera singer. B-but..."

Kotobuki confessed as if blaming herself, her voice wavering.

"Actually, I was a little bit nervous. I felt like Yuka was starting to get distant...S-so I hated it when she talked about her Angel of Music. I mean...Yuka sounded so happy when she was talking about the angel and would get so worked up, and it felt like she'd forgotten about me.

"I—*hk*...I was jealous of the angel the whole time, and I said mean things about him, so—maybe that's why Yuka didn't say anything when she went off to be with him."

As Kotobuki sobbed, it was like watching my old self.

My thoughts turned slowly back to the past in the dim darkness.

I had felt the same things Kotobuki was feeling.

Thinking that someone I loved was growing distant.

"I'm gonna be a writer. Tons of people are going to read my books."

"If anyone can be a writer, it's you, Miu. I'm behind you."

As she spread her wings toward her dreams, Miu was brilliant, and I loved her, and I proudly believed she could reach places higher than anyone else.

But at the same time my heart threatened to collapse under my anxiety—wondering what I would do if Miu became a real author and went away where I couldn't be with her.

The thing that pulled me back from being sucked into a mire of regret was the sound of feeble sniffling.

Beside me, Kotobuki choked back her voice, whining like a puppy.

This was no time to be thinking about things that happened long ago. I had to take Kotobuki back home.

She would catch cold if she stayed in a place like this too long.

But what could I...

"Kotobuki?"

The whining sobs went on. Her face stayed planted on her knees, too.

"There's a worm on your knee."

"Ack!!"

Kotobuki shrieked cutely and jumped, and in that moment, her footing slipped and she fell grandly to the floor.

"Ack! Sorry!"

After her butt slammed into the floor, Kotobuki glared at me tearfully.

"Grrr."

Uh-oh. She was angry.

As an awkward feeling pervaded the room, a black creature that gave rise to a tactile sensation scurried past Kotobuki.

"Oh...a cockroach."

"Eeeeek!"

Kotobuki let out an even louder scream than before and clung to me.

The smell of sweat and shampoo tickled my nose, and her slender arms wrapped tightly around my shoulders.

Kotobuki buried her small face in my chest and trembled.

"You don't like cockroaches, either, huh?"

"I-is there anyone who does...?!"

"Er, well..."

I didn't know what to say.

"Kotobuki."

"Ah!! What?!"

She pressed her face against my chest in terror.

Now what? But I probably ought to tell her.

"I can see your underwear."

Kotobuki whipped her face up and looked over her shoulder.

She could see that her skirt was flipped up past her hips and that her protruding bottom and striped underwear were in full view; then she released a voiceless shriek and pushed me away with both hands.

She swept her hands out to push her skirt down, looking like she was on the verge of tears; then she ran to the opposite corner of the room, turned her back on me, hugged her head in her arms, and crumpled into a ball.

"G-geez. I hate you so much. You're awful!"

"I...I'm sorry."

Maybe I should have fixed it on the sly after all. But I figured that if she caught me, I would look like a pervert...

In any case, I'd gotten an eyeful. White and pink stripes...

Oh...

Out of nowhere, in the flickering of the candles, a scene came to my mind.

That day when the cold wind of winter had gusted so powerfully.

Inside the gingko leaves dancing on the sidewalk. When I'd run breathless...

Could it be...?

I murmured a single breath only. "The school emblem...could it be..."

Yes—the golden leaves tumbling down, the familiar path continuing on to the library...

"Um, *did you tear your skirt?*"

Kotobuki, who had been groaning, her back hunched over, turned a bright red face toward me.

She pursed her lips, glared at me with angry, tear-filled eyes, and said, "Y-you're awful."

She groaned bitterly, then turned back toward the wall and curled into a ball again.

"Why...did seeing my underwear make you remember? You're *terrible!*"

So I was right.

That girl had been Kotobuki.

The winter of my second year of middle school.

Wearing a short coat over her uniform, that girl had strode past me looking like she was angry about something.

That day, stuff at school had run long, and I was in a rush because I was late for a meet up.

Miu was waiting for me at the library. I had to hurry.

But my eye was drawn to the fact that there was a gaping vertical tear in the girl's skirt, and I could see her pink-and-white striped underwear. Every time she boldly planted her foot, stripes flashed out of her gray pleated skirt.

Should I tell her?

But she'd probably be embarrassed if a boy told her...

As I struggled with this, the girl seemed to notice it herself. She dropped a hand to her rear and circled it up and down. Then she moved to a corner of the path, looking shocked.

She twisted her skirt around, then tried pinching the tear, stretching it out, and fixing it together, all while looking utterly baffled.

I remembered when the hem of Miu's skirt had frayed before, she would put it up with a safety pin as a quick fix, so I took the emblem off my uniform and moved toward the girl, holding it out to her.

"Um, maybe you don't need my help, but... you can pin up the tear with this. It's fine. It'll fool people for a little while."

I didn't remember the girl's face.

Given the situation, I thought it would be bad if I looked too closely at her, and I was embarrassed, too, so I probably couldn't meet her gaze head-on.

The girl looked like she was in a hurry, too, and I think she was groaning "huh?" and "ugh," keeping her face down.

I put my blue emblem in the shape of a maple into her hand, said, "See you," and ran off.

"You didn't remember the emblem...o-of all things...remembering...because of...my panties..."

Kotobuki turned her back on me stubbornly.

I didn't get the feeling that this would be a good time to explain my side of it. She seemed ready to spend the rest of the night grumbling.

Now what?

After turning it over in my mind, I opened my cell phone and called Kotobuki's number.

A cute love song by a female pop star played in Kotobuki's coat pocket.

Kotobuki stopped complaining and gulped.

Then she got her phone out and put it to her ear.

I could hear Kotobuki's dry, hesitant breathing through the earpiece.

"Hello? It's Inoue. I'd like to talk to Nanase Kotobuki. Is she available?"

I heard another gulp and her hesitant response.

"...Wh-what is it?"

I talked into the cell phone.

"First off, I'm sorry. You gave me hints and everything, and I never picked up on it. It's not that I didn't remember you. I just didn't look at your face very closely that day because I was embarrassed."

"Wh-whatever...it's no big deal. And I thought that might be it..."

"But what did you mean when you said you came to see me every day after that? We only met once, right?"

Tension ran through Kotobuki's back. A stuttering voice came over the phone punctuated by hesitant breathing.

"You...ran off without even telling me your name, though. I saw you go into the library, so I...wanted to...thank you...And after I pinned up my skirt, I went to the library...And...and you were talking to a girl with a ponytail, and it looked like you were having such a good time..."

Memories surfaced of those days when I would spend my time after school with Miu in the public libraries.

It was my daily routine to do homework there.

Kotobuki went on with her story, her voice hitching.

"You were sitting beside each other at a table and had a real casual look going on, so...I didn't want to bother you guys, so I couldn't say anything to you. But as soon as I got home, I regretted not thanking you.

"Then the next day, I went to the library. I wasn't sure if you'd be there, but...I thought I might as well try.

"When I got there, you were sitting at a table next to that girl again and laughing so happily, so...Every time after that, you were with her, always having fun, not seeing anything but her, and I couldn't find a good moment..."

Surprised, I asked, "You came to the library every day? To thank me?"

"I was stupid. It's like I was stalking you," Kotobuki spat, sounding annoyed at herself. Then her voice grew suddenly frail again. "A-and then—I'm sorry!...I wasn't trying to listen, but...I could hear what you guys were saying. So I heard your name, and I heard you call her Miu..."

I gasped.

"So you thought Miu was Miu Inoue?"

Kotobuki flinched.

Then keeping her phone pressed to her ear, she slowly turned to face me. She looked up at me with vulnerable eyes, like a child waiting to get scolded by the teacher.

"She was always writing stuff on loose-leaf paper and making you read it, though. And I accidentally overheard her say she was going to apply to the next Summer's Breeze new author competition... You told her she could be the youngest person to ever win the grand prize.

"So when the news started talking about a fourteen year-old middle schooler winning the prize, I thought I could feel my heart stop. She'd won. And after that, suddenly neither of you came to the library anymore. I thought that must be why..."

Kotobuki's face, her words, stirred up days long gone, and my heart squeezed tight with melancholy.

Miu doodling lightly on the back of my hand with a mechanical pencil and winking at me teasingly, her bouncing ponytail, her fresh, soapy scent.

Days of refreshing happiness.

"Konoha, do you like me? Look me in the eye and say it. Do you like me? Hmm? I love you. How much do you like me, Konoha?"

Miu always having fun and teasing me. *"You're special to me, Konoha. So I'm going to tell you and only you what my dream is."* She pressed her lips softly to my ear and whispered that to me.

I thought my brain would boil in that moment, my heart would burst, and my body would melt away.

"I'm thinking of applying to the Summer's Breeze new author competition. If I won the grand prize, they'd turn my story into a book. The youngest person to ever win was seventeen. I wanna win younger than that."

"If anybody can win the grand prize as the youngest person ever,

it's you, Miu. I can't wait for your story to be a book. I get your very first autograph. That's a promise."

Miu giggled and said I was getting ahead of myself.

Kotobuki had been there with us back then.

She'd been watching Miu and me that whole time.

Our innocent, happy hours—

A sharp pain welled up in my throat.

Of course, Kotobuki had misunderstood.

Miu had written a novel first. All that time, I'd done nothing more than read for Miu and started writing something that looked like a novel to imitate her, and I'd kept it a secret from her.

I hadn't had the slightest intention of being a fourteen-year-old girl genius as an author, and I'd never imagined that our happy lives could be shattered so easily.

It hurt to have Kotobuki, who had known me back then, watching me with such fragile eyes, so in a hoarse voice I said, "You got it wrong. Miu wasn't Miu Inoue. Miu Inoue wasn't her—"

Kotobuki kept her cell phone pressed to her ear and stared at me, as if awaiting my next words.

"Miu...Miu Inoue was..."

The words stuck in my throat, and my breathing grew more strained. The hand that held my phone grew cold.

Kotobuki asked in a small voice, almost like a sigh, "If she wasn't Miu Inoue...then what's she doing now?"

In that instant, a shock of pain that seemed to crush my heart in its grasp and a stormy vision, black as night, assaulted me.

A roof at the beginning of summer. A fluttering skirt and ponytail. Miu turning around with a sad face to smile at me. Her last words.

"You would never understand, Konoha."

139

Miu falling away backward. Myself screaming.

The world breaking apart like scattering puzzle pieces.

The heavy, firm portals of memory opened with a creak, and a voice filled with malice rang out cruelly.

"It's not that guys like you don't notice. You just don't want to know."

People like you or Miu Inoue hurt people and force them into corners naively.

No! Stop! I'm not the one who cornered Miu!

Ohhh, but—

An invisible hand crushed my heart in its grasp, my throat squeezed almost shut, and I could no longer breathe.

Wasn't I forgetting something important?

Hadn't I turned the lock on my heart any number of times so that I wouldn't remember?

"Inoue!"

Kotobuki stood up and ran over to me.

I knelt on the floor and took shallow breaths as I shuddered.

"What's wrong?! You're sweating so much..."

"...Ngh. I'm fine... Thanks."

"Sorry... this is 'cos I asked all that stuff."

"That's not true. It's not your fault."

I gave a misshapen smile with my dry lips to reassure Kotobuki, who looked like she was about to cry.

"I won't ever see Miu again. She moved away, and I haven't heard from her since..."

Kotobuki's face fell and she gulped.

Somehow I got my attack under control, but in its place a wrenching regret pressed down on my heart.

That day two years ago when Miu jumped off the roof, she escaped death's grasp.

The fact that there were bushes right under her and that she hit a pole on the way down meant the speed of the fall was lessened, which kept her alive.

But for a long time her condition was precarious, and no one but her family was allowed to see her at the hospital.

She finally regained consciousness, but even after therapy, problems persisted. When I found out that she wouldn't be able to walk or move her hands like she used to, I was thrust once more into darkness.

What was Miu feeling? Why had she jumped off the roof? Why had she said those things to me? What did she think of me now?

Was it my fault that Miu jumped—?!

I'd wanted to see Miu and hear what she had to say, but she wouldn't see me. I was also terrified of hearing the truth from Miu's mouth, terrified to the point of shaking. Every night I groaned at the dreams I had about Miu falling, and I would leap awake, throw up in the bathroom, and even if I went back to bed, I couldn't sleep and just spent the night tangling up the sheets.

I wanted to see Miu.

But I was scared.

I didn't want to see her. Every single day I went to the hospital feeling oppressed, and every time I went to the front desk and was informed that I couldn't see Miu, knives sliced into my heart and shredded it.

While that was going on, while I was still ignorant of the answers, Miu moved away. Nobody knew where she'd gone.

Miu disappeared without telling me anything.

After that, I had several attacks where I suddenly stopped being able to breathe. After I collapsed at school, I got taken to the hospital in an ambulance and ended up being a recluse.

In tears, I told the publishers who were pressing me for a sequel that I would never write another novel, that I couldn't write anything, that I hated novels and Miu Inoue, that I was Konoha Inoue, not Miu. I cut off all communication with them, and the author Miu Inoue disappeared from the world.

More than two years had gone by, and in that time I'd never gotten a single letter from Miu and heard no news of hear.

Because Miu had never fit in with the girls in my class, and she didn't have any other close friends...

I knew I would never see her again.

Miu had gone far away without ever forgiving me.

Kotobuki looked at me with a taut expression.

She was probably feeling bad because she thought she'd hurt my feelings. She rumpled her hair with one hand and spoke in a desperate, strained voice.

"I...I'm sorry...I don't know why I always say such nosy things...I'm offensive, and I dunno how I sound, so when I was in middle school all the boys said I had an awful personality and they hated me. The teachers thought I was rebelling against them, too, and they glared at me. God...I haven't changed at all. I hate this. All I ever wanted was to be a nice, sociable girl like Yuka."

Then she slumped.

"You don't have a bad personality, Kotobuki. You've got all those friends in our class, after all."

Keeping her eyes down, Kotobuki murmured in a thick voice, "That's—I got them all through Yuka...She's been helping me out and supporting me ever since middle school. She'd tell me, 'You should smile more, Nanase. That way people can tell that you're not mad.' She would always give me advice like that. But all I ever did was lean on her, and when she was in trouble, I couldn't do anything to help."

The faint light of the candles illuminated Kotobuki's sad face, orange flames flickering over her white cheeks.

Like me, Kotobuki had lost someone important to her.

Her life had been changed and suddenly lost.

I, too, knew the pain and the despair that seemed to rip your body apart when you faced it head-on.

Why?

How come?

Even though Miu had been smiling at me in what I know was happiness up until now.

Even though I believed that our peaceful, unassuming lives spent hand in hand would go on forever and ever, for eternity—

The questions repeating over and over deep in my heart that have no answers—the unending regrets, the incurable pain.

Kotobuki, who hugged her knees and hung her head now, was me two years ago.

But one thing was different.

Kotobuki hadn't lost Mito completely yet.

Just as Kotobuki was concerned about Mito, Mito was worried about Kotobuki, too. The fact that even after she had disappeared, she'd kept on sending Kotobuki messages and called me were obviously because she didn't want to hurt Kotobuki.

Kotobuki wasn't alone in her feelings. Mito cared about her, too.

Raoul was a noble-hearted, spoiled son of good upbringing, and he'd had no power to resist the Phantom.

But if Kotobuki and I incited some kind of action right now, the way Raoul had valiantly entered the subterranean kingdom, we might be able to tear Christine from the Phantom's grasp.

Though I wasn't sure whether I was fulfilling the role of the Persian who rescued Raoul.

We might still be in time.

Ah, but—going to the underground kingdom meant revealing the truth that Mito had kept hidden.

Kotobuki would find out what Mito had been doing up until she disappeared and what she was trying to do now. Could she accept the fact that the friend she was so proud of and who she loved had worked as an escort and had even threatened people in order to get a lead role?

Would Kotobuki be able to stay friends with her, however dark and ghastly Mito's "true" self was—however much of a stranger she was from the girl Kotobuki knew?

If it were me—

A sharp pain stabbed through my chest.

Did I want to know everything about Miu?

To know the truth about her?

Why did Miu jump that day? Why did she avoid me all of a sudden? Why did she stop talking to me? Why did she start going home without me? Why did she look daggers at me and unleash her hatred on me?

And the reason for that sad smile.

Did I want to know that?

No matter how intense the truth might be? Even if I was beset by suffering and despair even greater than I'd felt up till now, and it laid me out to the point that I couldn't get back up?

Even if I couldn't bear the pain and went crazy?

But learning the truth wasn't necessarily the right thing—

A battering voice thundered through my head.

"You just don't want to know. You're a coward and a hypocrite. You pretend to be a victim, then turn your eyes from the truth and keep on running."

My breath caught, and I almost collapsed at an intense pain like a red-hot iron bar being thrust into an open wound and shaken around.

Stop! Don't attack me anymore!

I'd finally managed to return to a peaceful life. I thought I'd be able to forget about Miu Inoue and start over. The truth wouldn't necessarily save you. You could sometimes be happier not knowing. Mr. Mariya had said that.

No, I didn't want to know! I didn't!

Even though I was in this much pain, I was so terrified of opening the door to the truth that all I could do was plug my ears, close my eyes, fall to my knees, and bear it.

I was so, so terrified of learning how Miu felt that I couldn't handle it. If I found out that Miu hated me, I knew I wouldn't be able to go on living—

As I wrestled with these thoughts, beside me Kotobuki buried her face in her knees and her shoulders trembled minutely.

What about Kotobuki—? What would she do? Did she want to know the truth about her best friend, even if the pain burrowing into her heart made her thrash in torment?

Kotobuki was in the same position I was, so she would understand this fear and anxiety that threatened to crush us in deep darkness, wouldn't she? We had both been hurt so much and we couldn't bear any further betrayal or hatred—

In a low voice, I asked, "Kotobuki...If...if Mito wasn't the kind of person you thought she was...would you want to know the truth?"

Kotobuki gasped and lifted her face to look at me.

"If...if Mito was a criminal or if she betrayed you...do you think you'd want to know?"

Kotobuki probably didn't understand why I was asking a question like that out of nowhere.

But she may have sensed something dark and murky that was implicit in my feeble, almost inaudible voice, my trembling lips, and my beseeching eyes. She looked up at me with a tense, uneasy face.

The flames flickered, the smell of smoke pricked my nose, and the air stabbed at my skin.

Kotobuki's face fell into a look of vulnerability as she murmured something.

"...I want to know. I want to save Yuka."

That instant—my heart swelled and I thought I might cry.

She had spoken the answer I'd been too afraid to give and as if it was the only logical choice.

Though in reality she was an ordinary girl who had no power to fight the Phantom, who was vulnerable and kind and headstrong and prone to tears, she had said she wanted to know, had said that she wanted to save Yuka.

I couldn't stop my heart from trembling at those simple, powerful words—tenderness and courage and prayers and a desire to protect all welled up in my chest one after another, and I hugged Kotobuki close.

Her small, chilled body trembled in my arms in surprise.

"I, Inoue—"

I wouldn't be swayed by Omi's words anymore.

The courage Kotobuki had shown roused me from my cowardice and pulled me to my feet.

Miu taught me that.

Now, I hugged Kotobuki tightly, as if to hold fast to this warm, certain object that I could touch.

"Let's...look for Mito together. Let me help again. Please, let me stay with you till the end."

Her small, fragile hands, which she stretched out hesitantly, closed tightly around my back.

Kotobuki nodded an okay, still sobbing.

The empty room that smelled of mold and smoke was lit by the faint candlelight.

We were very weak as we held each other, tears blurring our eyes, but I could believe that as long as we were together, we might grow stronger.

If Kotobuki was hurt by learning the truth later on, I would support her when it happened.

I would witness the truth about Mito with Kotobuki until the end, without turning my eyes from it.

"I'm sure Mito will be back by Christmas. She'll keep her promise to you. Let's try to believe that for now."

"Yeah...okay..."

Hot tears dropped from her eyes and soaked my neck as Kotobuki nodded over and over.

"Thank you. And for giving me...your emblem. Thank you...I've wanted to thank you for so long...I've wanted to tell you I appreciated it...This whole time...I've been watching you."

Then still crying, she murmured quietly, "You...were my first love."

<hr/>

Where did I stray from the path?

Neither the singing that resounds to the ceiling nor the applause of the audience makes me happy; they've only brought about disaster.

If I hadn't wanted something so intangible that vanished like a soap bubble, the Phantom never would have gotten the better of me.

Talent wasn't something I needed.

That pure, kind sensation I felt when I turned the pages of Miu Inoue's book. The peaceful warmth of the every day.

Going to school like everyone else, talking to friends, studying, eating lunch.

Waiting after school and then going home together, studying together at the library...laughing.

Exchanging presents on Christmas Eve and promising that we would be together forever...tangling our fingers together...

A perfectly unassuming life like that would have been fine...

I was content just feeling the tenderness that surged up in me like sunlight when I touched his hand and with my bounding happiness when I saw Nanase smile.

Nanase—Nanase.

What are you doing right now? What's on your mind?

I'm thinking about you, Nanase. You're the only thing I have left that's important to me.

I hope you're happy. I hope all of your wishes come true.

The truth is, I hate Miu Inoue. I've always hated her. No, that's not true. It's just when I see a world that's too beautiful, I feel it crushing my chest and I can't turn the pages because of the pain.

I took off my ring.

I can't ever go back.

The light of the sun is too blinding for me.

I can't help but loathe those who dirtied me and cast me into darkness.

I will have my revenge on them.

I'll put on a mask and become a Phantom, chase them down, corner them, seal them up in a labyrinth of illusions, torment them relentlessly, then deliver the coup de grace.

Even if they prayed for forgiveness, it would be far too late for that. Let them be spattered in humiliation, be spattered in corruption; let them hear the dirge that spills from my lips, once those of a human being but no longer.

The angel who deceived me, the men who treated me like an animal, you've all made me into a Phantom.

Curse you—curse all of you!

Chapter 6—A Song of Ice and Death

That evening, Kotobuki and I went home hand in hand.

I told her about Mito as we walked slowly, leisurely down the dark road, and Kotobuki kept her eyes downcast the entire time, taking it in.

Occasionally, I felt her hand flinch faintly in my grasp. Every time I tightened my fingers around hers to reassure her, and when I did, she would timidly squeeze back.

When we parted ways in front of her house, Kotobuki said, her eyes red, "I believe that I'm going to spend Christmas with Yuka again this year. She's still going to be my best friend for a long time."

I still hadn't heard anything from Mr. Mariya.

"There's nothing to worry about. It's Marmar, after all. He'll just come back looking indifferent," Shoko said with a rueful smile. I'd met up with her in the coffee shop near the academy.

"Marmar isn't bound by things like common sense or money or honor. When he was a student, while everyone else was desperately aiming for the top, he was always standing at the pinnacle, perfectly aloof. And despite that, he threw it away like it was nothing."

She dropped the hand that held her cigarette from her mouth, and her look turned envious.

"I...wish I could live like he does."

She played it off with a joke about how hard it was to be a teacher, and then Shoko told me how things were going at the school.

"We're doing rehearsals with the understudy right now. Mito is still the lead, but...if she doesn't show up on the day of the performance, the understudy will probably go onstage."

And then Maki showed me a video of Mr. Mariya from when he won the competition abroad. He stood on the stage wearing a black tuxedo, belting out his cheerful singing with a sunny expression on his face.

Maki rested an elbow on her crossed knees and looked absorbed in his performance.

"He's amazing at holding the high notes. He used to sing with a choir when he was little, you know. They said he had the voice of an angel. I've heard CDs of his from back then, and his voice is a beautiful, pure soprano—like a little bell."

My heart skipped a beat when she said the word *angel*.

A bewitching smile came over Maki's lips.

"The art world will occasionally give rise to unprecedented monsters. That's why I'm not interested in it...But he may have been nicknamed as an ageless, sexless angel because from the Western perspective, Asians seem not to age."

Sexless...Something not masculine and also not feminine. It was true that there was something androgynous about Mr. Mariya. Could he also be Mito's angel?

"In any case, if Yuka Mito is a singer who's been selected by an Angel of Music, I would definitely expect her to be at the recital."

Perhaps Maki knew something, but I didn't expect someone as formidable as her to reveal anything.

Omi had been out of school all that time. Kotobuki had told me, "Omi has never been very healthy," but of course, I couldn't see it that way.

At the very least, I suspected he had some sort of connection to Mr. Mariya. I also still wondered how he'd known that I was Miu Inoue.

"That reminds me, Kotobuki—have you gotten any weird messages? Mori told me that when you were in the nurse's office before you said something about the Phantom."

Kotobuki's cheeks reddened and she grew suddenly flustered.

"Th-that was...because I got this chain letter thing that was bad luck, and I got really scared. I just crossed it with the Phantom in my mind. People play that trick all the time, but I guess I got a little nervous. I'm fine now!"

I didn't think that could be the only reason she'd gotten so scared, but...I admired how she pursed her lips and tried to look strong, and I wanted to protect her through everything.

Would Mito appear at the recital after all—?

Christmas was right around the corner, too.

Tohko rested her index finger on her lips and bent her ear to my story with a serious expression; then she lamented, "I have the National Center Test on Sunday."

"Are you still trying for a national school?"

"Of course."

"Then forget about the recital, and study your butt off."

"Hey, why are you *sighing*? Geez, I'm going to get a C next, you'll see!"

"You think that makes you safe?"

In this way, we came to the day of the performance.

The city was wall-to-wall Christmas. Christmas songs played on the streets, and even the people walking there seemed somehow excited, having fun.

The concert started at eleven, and we arrived at a hall on the academy's campus thirty minutes early. Even though it was only a student recital, the spacious lobby was decorated with flower arrangements with placards on them, and the reception desk was piled high with bouquets as well.

Kotobuki also hugged a bouquet of bright blue roses to her chest.

"Those roses are superblue. I've never seen that color before."

"They're Yuka's favorite flowers," Kotobuki said, sounding slightly embarrassed. "I bought them online. It's not their real color. They dye white roses blue. They're supposed to stand for the blessing of God."

Today, Kotobuki was wearing a maxi dress with a ribbon on it and a billowing coat over that. It might have been her clothes that made her look more graceful and cuter than usual.

"The blessing of God, huh? That's a good thing to represent."

"Yeah, Yuka said that on her seventeenth birthday, her boyfriend gave her these roses. She was so happy. She took a ton of pictures of them with her cell phone and sent them to me."

"I'm sure they'll make her happy again."

"I...hope so."

We had the receptionist call Shoko, and she came out looking extremely harried.

"Mito's still not here," she said in a bitter tone.

She had dark circles under her eyes, and her skin tone was

muted. She looked a little annoyed. Backstage they were probably waiting for Mito's appearance with soul-crushing anxiety.

We said we would come back after the performance, then left Shoko.

"We'll be able to see Mito backstage once the recital is over. Then we'll give her the flowers," I said.

"...Okay."

Kotobuki was probably disappointed. She nodded with a cheerless look. The blue roses she held in her arms swayed slightly each time she took a step.

Our seats were in the first row of the second level.

Was Mr. Mariya here? Or Omi?

I tried scanning the audience, but there were way too many people and I couldn't tell.

At last the announcement to turn off our cell phones played, the hall grew dark, and a bell rang announcing the start of the performance.

The opera *Turandot* had begun.

The daughter of a Chinese emperor, Turandot has a cruel nature, and she presents three riddles to the men who come to seek her hand, and if they fail to answer them correctly, she cuts off their heads. The nomad prince Calaf, driven from his country by war, is present for the execution of a Persian prince, and he feels a powerful wrath at the icelike princess.

However, his heart is captured immediately thereafter by the beauty of the princess who appears in the tower, and heedless of those around him trying to prevent it, he begs to marry the princess and solve her riddles.

The man playing Calaf was a guest performer, a professional opera singer. With the emperor's palace steeped in the light of sunset as his backdrop, his vibrant tenor rang out youthfully, like a trumpet.

"My entire body is aflame...
My every sense is violent torture!
Every string of my heart
Holds fast to one word and shouts it,
Turandot! Turandot! Turandot!"

Wow!

The acoustics might be having an effect, but I'd had no idea a human voice could scale so high. It really was like a musical instrument!

The song was in Italian, but I'd learned the story ahead of time so I could pretty much tell what the scene was. The singer made the range of his emotions almost painfully clear, and the character's feelings rode the music and bit into my chest with overwhelming force.

Turandot's debut was still a ways off. Would Mito appear on the stage?

I felt a pinched pain at my temples, and my impatience made the time feel longer.

Still holding the blue roses, Kotobuki's eyes were fixed on the stage and her look was one of prayer.

When the first act ended and we moved on to the second, the backdrop changed to that of the castle interior.

There were the wails of ministers being twisted about by the princess's whims. There were people gathered in the courtyard of the castle interior. There was an exchange between the emperor and Calaf.

When the emperor orders him to leave the palace immediately, Calaf sings out decisively in response.

"Son of heaven, I beg of you!
  Let me attempt this test!"

It would be soon.
  Sweat covered the palms of my hands, and my breathing grew strained.
  Soon Turandot would appear.
  At the tall staircase in the center of the stage.
  A spotlight fell on its summit, and the chorus sang.

"Princess, I beg you, show yourself!
  Let the world be radiant!"

Kotobuki leaned forward. I forgot to even blink as I stared at the staircase. I was convinced that Turandot would appear there for the competition.
  But Turandot didn't show herself.
  The rest of the audience must have thought it was strange. A buzz spread like a wave.
  Mito was late—!
  Just then, a pure high note rang out from an unexpected direction.
  Behind the seating on the first floor.
  From there, a girl advanced down the center aisle toward the stage.
  A majesty that frosted the very air emanated from the maiden, who wore a gorgeous thin silk robe of red and gold that trailed behind her and a large golden crown on her head over her beautiful, long black hair.
  The slaughtering princess, Turandot!

The audience stirred.

The top half of Turandot's face was perfectly obscured by a white mask.

But all confusion was soon swept away by the singing of the diva, which dominated the hall.

A voice that glistened like transparent wings, stretching out and soaring to the most distant corners of the sky!

A rich and powerful high note rang out with enough energy to break down the walls of the theater or the doors to the lobby without weakening an iota in its terrifying power.

"In this palace, a thousand years now past,
    A scream of despair echoed here!"

"And that scream passed through the children and the grandchildren,
    To lodge itself here, in my soul!"

It was a voice truly beyond human comprehension! It was a song of utmost superiority and bliss performed by the instrument of heaven.

The bloody princess, the princess they called death, the ice princess. But still her voice glittered transparently like light pouring down from the sky, still it had a strength like steel and raised the girl Turandot from a gory butcher to a white, unsullied position of supremacy.

A chaste, ruthless, beautiful maiden who human men were not permitted to touch.

When she reached the center of the stage, the spotlight covered her in light, and she sent out her voice—high, clear, and crazed—to every corner of the hall.

Proclaiming that in order to avenge an ancestor, a princess who was dragged away and violated by the king of a foreign land long ago, her body would belong to no man.

"I will take my revenge against them,
    For the cry of that pure and stainless person,
    And for her death!"

"I would that none should win me!
    The animosity for the man who murdered that person
    Is raw in my heart!"

"No! No! I would that none should win me!"

How high could her voice go?!
    The higher the note became, the more her power increased, and her wings beat freely toward heaven.
    I hadn't studied singing or anything, and I didn't know much about opera, but there was no doubt that this voice was dragging the entire theater into a fevered, imagined whirlpool.
    Calaf's voice tangled with Turandot's.
    The high notes of the female soprano and the male tenor coursed fiercely up to the ceiling, as if each was trying to force the other to surrender.
    Even when Calaf's voice broke off, Turandot's voice continued stretching even higher, as if to make the difference in their power clear.
    The second act was over in the blink of an eye.
    Calaf gave exactly the right answers to the three questions Turandot posed.
    Even so, Turandot tried to reject Calaf's love. Calaf, therefore, posed a riddle to her in return, to guess his name by morning.
    If she guesses his name, he will die.

"You do not know my name, lady!
  Tell me my own name
  By dawn's light!
  If you do so, I will die!"

Turandot accepted.

The curtain fell, and the hall was enveloped in explosive applause and praise.

The audience sprang up, seemingly intoxicated.

The announcement of a twenty-minute intermission was lost in a storm of applause, and I could only hear snatches of it.

Kotobuki stood up, her face ashen.

"I—I have to go backstage! I can't wait for the opera to be over."

With a tight sense of dread, I headed toward the backstage door with Kotobuki.

Even if they wouldn't let us inside, if she could just find out about Mito—

But when we got there, the place was in chaos.

Staff members were running in and out of a gaping door, shouting loudly to each other.

"You still haven't found Mito?!"

"No! She wasn't in the bathroom or the lobby!"

"How could the lead actress abandon the stage and disappear?!"

"Watanabe, be ready to go on just in case."

"O-okay!"

Surprised, we looked at each other.

Mito had disappeared again!

The very next moment, we'd started running.

We had to look for Mito! She might still be in the area.

Where? Where could she have gone?

As we pounded blindly down the hallways of the theater, I shouted, "Kotobuki, try calling Mito's cell phone!"

With the bouquet in her arms, Kotobuki got her cell phone out of a pocket and busily moved her fingers.

Petals as blue as the ocean drifted to the floor.

"It's no good, she's not answering!" Kotobuki wailed.

Just then—

I caught the sound of a familiar Christmas song.

It was "Santa Claus Is Coming to Town."

Kotobuki gasped.

In a daze, we ran in the direction we heard the music coming from.

Petals cascaded to the floor. The lighthearted melody went on playing without interruption.

It came from the door in front of us!

When we turned the knob and burst in, we found a supply room. There were stacks of cardboard boxes and shelves on either side.

In the middle of it all, a masked girl wearing a brilliantly colored silk robe writhed around, both her hands trying to rip off a black scarf that was coiled around her neck.

We saw someone behind the girl, strangling her, and we gaped.

What was *she* doing here?

The masked girl's feet slipped, and she grabbed a corner of one of the shelves with one hand. The edge of her crown rang out and her red robe fluttered. The plain black scarf bit sharply into her slender neck and pulled taut with tension behind her. Strained gasps escaped the girl's lips.

"Stop!!"

Kotobuki threw down her bouquet of roses and launched herself at the person strangling Mito. I hung on to her other arm to stop her.

"Don't interfere!"

The person who spun around to face us, her breathing ragged and her face warped with insanity, was Shoko Kagami.

"I even took you under my wing! You told me your family was in trouble, so I sent you good clients! But still you betrayed me!"

Shoko was seriously worked up and seemed to not even register that we were there.

Her beautiful almond eyes glinted with hatred and rage. Her face was flushed dark red as she ground her teeth and yanked on the ends of the scarf.

Why?! Why did Shoko have so much loathing for Mito?

What did she mean she sent clients to her?

No—!

My voice seemed to tear at my throat as I shouted, "Shoko! *You were the one who introduced Mito to working as an escort!*"

Shoko's hand slipped from the end of the scarf, and she fell backward.

Kotobuki let out a shriek as our rear ends smacked into the floor simultaneously.

Shoko hit a shelf hard with her back, and she groaned. Leaning back against it, her shoulders heaving as she breathed, she spoke in a low voice.

"That's right...I did. After all, that's how I earned the money to continue my own musical education."

Kotobuki gasped.

Ignoring the hair that had fallen across her face, her eyes flashing eerily, Shoko continued. "You need money to do music. Not just for class fees, but for costumes, textbooks, the tickets for concerts you need to attend...And you burn up money to pay for private lessons outside of school or to study abroad. No matter how much you have, it's never enough.

"So I introduced the girls whose poverty was causing them problems to a pretty good job. I created a website and brought together clients I could trust."

Shoko had been the one running the site!

My body trembled at that fact. Kotobuki's jaw was tensed, too, her eyes wide.

"But you know, even after selling themselves to continue their studies, not a single girl succeeded as a musician. Every last one of them fell through, crumbled, got disappointed, and gave up on their dreams. Just like I did."

Shoko bit down on her lip ruefully and her face contorted; then her eyes grew even sharper.

"So how did you learn to sing like that?! *How?*

"When you sang the aria for the Queen of the Night in front of everybody, I couldn't believe it. It was amazing. I was astounded. *This girl is different from me, and from all those other girls. She might succeed.* As soon as the thought crossed my mind, it scared me, and I hated you more than I could stand!"

Her dark gaze, glinting harshly, held Mito in its grasp as she crouched against the wall. Shoko's dry lips spat out her bitterness.

"All the Camellias have to lose hope! Like I did, the very first Camellia! You can't be the only Camellia who's special. I won't let you. It isn't fair!"

Her fingers closed around a pair of large shears that were on a shelf, and Shoko leaped at Mito.

"Yuka! Look out!" Kotobuki screamed.

The scissors struck the wall right next to Mito's face and produced a shower of sparks.

Shoko growled spitefully and swung the scissors up again.

"You have no right to wear such beautiful clothes or to stand in the center of the stage!!!"

"*Stop!!*"

Kotobuki ran over but was sent flying by one of Shoko's elbows.

"Kotobuki!"

The scissors sliced off one side of Mito's wig.

The jet-black hair slithered to the floor like a snake. Shoko tugged on one of Mito's sleeves with all her might, ripping it away to reveal a white shoulder and arm.

"You've betrayed all of us! All of the other Camellias!"

Shoko's energy was terrible; I couldn't get near her.

Just then, behind Shoko, I could see a man in a suit standing near the door.

Mr. Mariya!

From there, he might be able to pin Shoko from behind.

Even if he couldn't do that, maybe he could call someone—!

But Mr. Mariya didn't move.

He was watching this tragic scene with a frigid, coldhearted gaze.

Coldly expressionless, as if he were wearing a mask over his face—!

Why?! Why wasn't he moving?!

Shoko shoved Mito to the floor, then sat astride her and started tearing at her clothes, deranged.

"You don't deserve a costume like this! No matter how you make yourself up, Camellia will never be more than a filthy whore! You and I are both corrupted beyond recognition!"

Her thin robe tore apart with a sharp *rrrip* and exposed her bare skin.

Her white throat—her chest—her hip—!

We all stared at Mito in disbelief.

Her clothes had been hiding not the supple body of a girl, but the firm body of a boy!

"No…"

Shoko's hands dropped, senseless. Her face, which had been twisted with hatred, reflected her violent confusion.

"What is this?! When did you change places? Where did Mito go?!"

Just then, the voice of someone who shouldn't have been there sounded from near the door.

"The Phantom knows that."

Slipping past Mr. Mariya, who stood agape, her long thin braids swaying, her head held proud, the person who entered the room was Tohko, wearing a navy-colored coat over her school uniform.

Chapter 7—Inside the Dark, Dark Earth

"What are you doing here? What about your test?"

I'd been thrown off guard. Tohko's cheeks flushed very slightly in response, and she murmured an excuse.

"I'm sorry. I was worried...so I ran out in the middle of it."

I felt dizzy for a moment. She was taking her exams soon and had gotten Fs. What was she thinking?!

Tohko opened her right hand, and blue petals fluttered out of it.

"When I followed these petals, I found you guys."

Mr. Mariya and Kotobuki were both gaping.

Shoko stood up and glared at Tohko.

"Who are you?"

Tohko puffed up her thin chest and answered crisply, "I am, as you see, a book girl."

That introduction was probably beyond the reach of Shoko's understanding. Her eyes went round, her mouth hung half open, and she stood speechless.

An awkward silence filled the cramped room.

Shoko finally returned to her senses, wrinkled up her face, and forced out a gasping question.

"You said the Phantom would know. What does that mean? Who is this boy?"

The masked boy in the ragged costume was huddled on the floor, a total mess, not even covering his naked chest.

Yeah—who *was* this kid?

To our confusion, Tohko breezily declared, "It would take some time to explain that, because this story featuring a girl named Yuka Mito involves a great many emotions and speculations, and the main plot has gotten obscured.

"But since it seems that a replacement will be going onstage, there's no longer any need for him to go back. We have plenty of time, so I think I'll unravel this story like a book girl should."

It was as if some strange power controlled the space we all occupied.

Shoko, Mr. Mariya, Kotobuki—all held their breath and watched Tohko as she began to tell the story in a voice as clear as water.

"This incident began with a situation that reminded me of Gaston Leroux's *Phantom of the Opera*.

"Leroux was a French man born in 1868, and after being active as a lawyer and journalist, he changed careers in his thirties to become an author, and he published a succession of stories, such as *The Mystery of the Yellow Room*, which is a famous closed-room mystery story. Maurice Leblanc of the Arsène Lupin series was active around the same time in France, and Leroux was a popular author whom many said was on the same level.

"In 1910, Leroux published *Le Fantôme de l'Opéra—The Phantom of the Opera*—describing a masked man living below the opera, and the way people got tangled up in his dark passions.

"Mito loved this story and had talked about wanting her own Angel of Music for a long time.

"Then like the heroine Christine, she took lessons from a certain figure in secret and he made her talent as a diva blossom.

"And Mito also had a man for the position of Raoul, Christine's lover.

"Mito didn't even reveal the man's name or identity to her best friend Nanase, though he was at Seijoh Academy. Instead, she offered three hints about him."

Tohko slowly raised a finger.

"One, there are nine people in his family.

"Two, he likes coffee.

"Three, whenever he's thinking about something, he's in the habit of walking around a desk.

"You would think saying that there are nine people in his family would be a major clincher, wouldn't you?

"But this hint does not actually refer to her boyfriend."

Tohko had said that before, too. That she didn't think Mito's boyfriend had nine people in his family...

As we all listened transfixed, Tohko gave the name of a book.

"There's a children's book called *The Pfaffling Family*. It's an old book and it's out of print in Japan, so people nowadays might not know about it. It was published in 1906. The author was Agnes Sapper, a German writer. Sapper, who was the mother of five children, wrote about the heartwarming lives of the mother, the father, and the seven children of the Pfaffling family.

"The father in this story is a little short-tempered, but he's described as a jolly, forthright character that we can love. He loves coffee, but the family is poor so he drinks it only on holidays. Also whenever he's thinking about something, he strides restlessly around a table, so he gets admonished by the woman who boards with them."

Tohko's voice was filled with strength.

"A family of nine, liking coffee, and walking around tables— all of these match the hints Mito gave. I heard that Mito used to read a lot of foreign children's novels about families, so there's no doubt in my mind that she knew about this one, too. So what was Mito trying to convey with these hints? The father of the Pfaffling family worked *as a music teacher.*"

Her wise eyes stared straight at Mr. Mariya.

"The reason Mito was keeping his name a secret was because he was a teacher, not a student. Even if he was at a different school, she thought that if the romance between a teacher and a high school student got out, it might cause trouble for him. As far as male music teachers at Seijoh Academy go—you're the only one, Mr. Mariya, which means you are Mito's Raoul."

The air was coldly tense.

Mr. Mariya wasn't Mito's angel—he was her lover!

Shoko's eyes widened in amazement, and Kotobuki trembled, her face ghostly white.

Mr. Mariya's eyes flashed with apparent annoyance and he spoke. His voice lacked its usual mildness, and his tone was curt.

"Yes—it's exactly as you've surmised. I was dating Yuka Mito. But I haven't seen her lately, and she hasn't contacted me. Perhaps she's found some other man that she likes? The 'angel' that she was taking her lessons with, for example. Yuka would talk about nothing but him, even if it had been a long time since I'd last seen her."

A murky anxiety steadily tightened in my chest.

Why was Mr. Mariya talking about his lover with such frigid eyes? It was as if he was talking about something he hated, something he was contemptuous of.

He was like a totally different person from the teacher who had smiled at us kindly in the music room!

"Is that why you were jealous of the angel?" Tohko asked. "The way Raoul felt uneasy about the ties between Christine and her Angel of Music, so that it burned fiercely in him…

"Nanase has testified that Mito was troubled because her boyfriend told her to quit her night work, and he was calling her a lot.

"You were frantic with worry that Mito was being drawn in by the angel, weren't you, Mr. Mariya? You couldn't forgive her for talking about another man in front of you, could you?"

"I think you've said enough! What you're saying is pure conjecture!"

His sharp yell rent the air and I flinched.

Mr. Mariya was glaring at Tohko murderously. Tohko took his look head-on, and in a strong voice that refused to bend to him, she responded, "That's right, I'm simply a book girl! I'm not a police officer or a detective, and everything I say is nothing more than my imagination. But I think that the way you acted after Mito disappeared was unnatural. This lover you were so obsessed with suddenly disappeared, so why didn't you search for her openly? Why did you ask Nanase to organize those files? Why did you deliberately show her your ticket to the recital?

"And you also went to a hotel with a first-year girl, and you walked around the room as if you were looking for something, and you wouldn't stop staring at the table, and then you left her there and went home alone—"

As soon as Tohko mentioned Sugino, I saw shock run across Mr. Mariya's face.

Tohko interrogated him tenaciously.

"Why were you looking at the table so intently, Mr. Mariya? What were you remembering while you stared at it?"

Something at the core of my body trembled at the very thought of this.

A bleak shadow was steadily closing in behind me.

"There was something you absolutely had to get back to the room to check on, wasn't there? Nanase said that the day Mito disappeared, she sent a message that she'd gotten a last-minute job and she had to go. That job was to go out with men for money—an underage escort.

"You'd been keeping an eye on her because you suspected her of cheating on you, and you discovered her secret, didn't you? And that day you met Mito at the hotel as a customer, *and you, Mito's Raoul, your jealousy and rage transformed you into the Phantom, and you knocked Mito's head into the table.*"

"No!!"

Mr. Mariya's voice cut into Tohko's words. His face twisted, his hands and legs trembled weakly, and confusion intermingled dizzyingly with violent emotion in his bloodshot eyes.

The shadow—the shadow was changing the color of the air.

"Yuka fell down all on her own! I told her to stop singing, but she wouldn't listen. Why did she have to continue with music if it meant doing something so shameful?!

"But Yuka cried and told me that singing was all she had left. She said the angel was waiting and she had to go to her lesson, and she turned her back on me, and she tried to leave the room!"

I was astounded.

It seemed that Mr. Mariya wasn't aware of what he was shouting. He kept on yelling as if his judgment had slipped loose.

"I lost my temper and strangled Yuka. Then we started struggling after that, and Yuka's foot slipped, and she hit her head on the edge of the table. She was bleeding and lying on the floor, and she stopped moving. I was so startled that I ran out of the hotel without her."

171

There was the sound of a heavy clatter as the scissors fell from Shoko's hand. She put both her hands to her mouth to hold back a scream.

Kotobuki was clinging to the edge of a shelf, her face pale as well.

I couldn't believe it, either—didn't want to believe it. How could Mr. Mariya have done something like that to Mito?!

Despite our confusion, Mr. Mariya continued his transformation before our eyes. His true face, twisted by jealousy and madness, appeared beneath his mask, and his voice, which had been sweetly cheerful, now cracked jarringly like a toad's.

"The next day there was no story on the news about a body being found in a hotel. And when I called Yuka's cell phone, I couldn't get ahold of her. So I pretended to be a family member and asked about her at school, which is when I found out that she'd been missing classes without permission and hadn't been back to the dorms. I thought I was going to lose my mind. Where had Yuka gone? Was she alive? Was she dead?"

That was when the tickets to the recital had come under the name Camellia.

The surprise Mr. Mariya had felt then came through painfully in his broken voice.

The reason he had kept Kotobuki nearby under the pretext of organizing files was so that he could keep an eye on her because he knew she was Mito's best friend and he suspected that Mito might contact her. And he'd shown her the recital tickets in order to see how Kotobuki would react.

Beneath his placid face, Mr. Mariya had been watching our movements closely, all while frantic, writhing, and suffering.

Mr. Mariya was Raoul and the Phantom!

In a turbulent, quavering voice, he went on.

"I received several messages on my cell phone and computer

from Camellia with words like *murderer* and *fallen angel*. But still she wouldn't come to me in person. She was in a mood to torment me slowly. I'm sure the angel was manipulating Yuka. The angel had taken her away from there.

"Yes, everything—everything!—is the angel's fault!

"If Yuka hadn't been drawn in by the angel—if she hadn't betrayed me—

"I wanted to save Yuka from the angel! But *I wasn't in time.* Yuka had been dragged into the angel's empire underground!"

The sight of Mr. Mariya shouting, his pupils dilated, threatened to tear my heart open.

I was sure that Mr. Mariya hadn't meant to hurt Mito.

The person he hated wasn't Mito; it was the angel who had stolen her heart.

Mr. Mariya probably didn't know that Mito's parents had committed suicide, either. Maybe he hadn't even heard about the loans.

So he hadn't understood how Mito felt.

Mito had wanted to continue her music even to the point of becoming an escort, and unable to comprehend that, he'd blamed the fact that she had changed on the angel and despised him.

And wasn't the reason he had gone to the hotel with Sugino because he regretted abandoning Mito there and just wanted to see if she was alive or dead?

Hadn't he tried to save her in his own way? That was why he'd stared at the table and muttered so grimly.

That he *wasn't in time*—

No, Mr. Mariya wasn't a bad person, and he wasn't a fallen angel. He was—he was—

Just then, a frigid voice echoed through the room.

"It wasn't me who betrayed her. You did that, Keiichi."

173

A high, clear girl's voice.

It was the masked boy who had spoken in a beautiful voice like ice, clothed in the torn costume and standing against the wall.

"Yuka...!" Kotobuki whispered, her face taut. Shoko, too, was watching his mouth as if she'd seen a monster.

Tohko pressed her lips together and stood firm, her expression grim, and I felt as if a cold hand was stroking my cheek.

His voice sounded exactly like Mito's, the voice I'd heard on the phone.

A high, clear girl's voice that no boy could have possessed after his voice changed—

Mr. Mariya's face twisted wildly, as if he was letting out a soundless scream of terror.

Like the ancestor reawakening inside Turandot, the princess of slaughter, it was as if Mito's soul had inhabited the boy's body in that instant and he spoke to Mr. Mariya with Mito's voice.

"You killed me; my body is rotting in the cold ground."

A chill ran through my entire body.

What in the world was happening? Was this real?

"That's a lie!" Mr. Mariya yelled as sweat poured off of him. "There was no body at the hotel! Yuka's not dead. She's alive and with the angel!"

The girl's voice reverberated coldly like sharp icicles.

"You've always been like this, Keiichi. You try to justify your actions and stay clean. *That day*, too, you attacked me for being a corrupted woman, and you tried to kill me."

"I didn't..."

"Yes, you did," her voice proclaimed coolly. "While you strangled me, your eyes glinted like blades with the hatred and murderous intent of your wounded pride. Just like they do now."

Mr. Mariya was speechless with surprise.

"When I fell down and stopped moving, you left me behind and you ran. Afterward, when I woke up, I cleaned up the blood that had spilled on the floor... You can't possibly imagine how that felt, since you thought only about protecting yourself.

"Or how it felt to sneak out of the hotel.

"Or how it felt to walk down the street at night, buffeted by the cold wind...

"Or what I thought about as I passed away the next morning, drawing my last breath in my sleep...

"The cause of *my death* was a contusion to the head.

"Are you still going to claim that you didn't kill me?"

Mr. Mariya's lips quivered, and he wrung a muffled voice from the back of his throat. But it didn't form into words.

Kotobuki watched the boy who told the story of her best friend's death in the girl's own voice with a frightened, confused look.

Were the things he was saying true?

Had Mito drawn her last breath the morning after she met Mr. Mariya at the hotel?

My throat twitched, and the core of my brain grew numbingly hot.

If that was true, what would Kotobuki do? She had been waiting for Mito, trusting that she would come home for Christmas!

The masked boy slowly raised his slender hand and pointed at Mr. Mariya.

Like Turandot, who sang that she would never forgive the crimes of men, he cold-bloodedly declared in a high, clear voice, "You are an arrogant Lucifer. Killing me is not your only crime.

175

"*You taught me the wrong way to sing, and you tried to crush my throat. Didn't you,* Keiichi?"

The greatest shock of all ran over Mr. Mariya's face.

We all gasped in surprise as well.

He'd tried to crush Mito's throat! That—that would mean—

"No! I was—"

From behind the white mask, a knife blade of a gaze thrust into Mr. Mariya as he retreated, utter terror in his eyes.

The voice, which made us feel its rage, railed mercilessly against Mr. Mariya, condemning him.

"You weren't jealous only of my relationship with my angel! *You were jealous of my talent, too!* You loathed me and the angel who made my talent bloom, loathed us more than you could bear, and so you killed me!"

Mr. Mariya swung his head up.

"That's not true! I hated that Yuka was consumed with singing.

"Yes, she had a good voice. But there's no shortage of people like that in the world, and even if by some stroke of luck she succeeded, it would only be a temporary thing. She would lose it again soon enough and would be forced to experience heartrending disappointment. That much was certain. I was the same way!" he screamed fearsomely.

He spoke, shaking, and his expression was tortured, filled with a fierce pain.

"When I was a child, they called me an angel and played me up as a genius. But then my voice changed, and though my technique was excellent, as soon as I got my adult voice, people would blithely tell me that something was missing or that I'd lost the spark I'd had as a child.

"Even so, I struggled until I bled! Believing that someday I would develop a voice even more magnificent than the one I'd lost—

"That was when, during my study abroad in Paris, I heard the singing of a real angel."

What did that mean? Was there a singer besides Mr. Mariya who people had called an angel? But then, why a *real* angel?

Mr. Mariya's face warped awfully.

"That voice...! A pure voice that could never have come from a man whose voice had changed, which seemed to send beads of light tumbling from the stage—the clear, high voice I had lost—

"That voice—I realized as soon as I heard the song that what I desired was my lost soprano. That a tenor was nothing more than a parody of what I wanted."

Shoko cried out, her voice a scream, "How can you say that?! Your tenor was sweet and transparent and amazing! You even won competitions and managed to work as a professional. Everyone envied you!"

For Shoko, who had sold her body to pay her school fees and had still been incapable of succeeding as a singer, who had gotten her revenge by corrupting her students—for Shoko, Mr. Mariya's talk must have been such a shock that it couldn't help but push her over the edge.

For Shoko, Mr. Mariya must have been a symbol of talent, standing effortlessly at the pinnacle she could never reach.

"I would have cast off that wretched tenor for anything. It was worthless! It was pure luck that I won the contests! If only I'd had my old soprano! If I could have sung the way I did then, but no—"

Mr. Mariya furrowed his brows tightly in pain and forced the words out.

"Even... *even when I was a boy—I never could have sung like that.* It wasn't my tenor that was the parody, it was me. Confronted by a voice like that, I was nothing more than a counterfeit angel, and now that I was an adult, I would never be able to surpass that voice again. It was a complete defeat; there could be no better.

"When I realized that, I felt as if I had been cast from a cliff.

"Still I couldn't stop myself from seeking out that beautiful voice! Frequenting the concerts, I heard that voice many times. And each time I despaired. I wanted it to pardon me already. That everlasting pain—the thing I hated most in the world—was the very thing that I couldn't help but love more than anything in the world, and I wanted the voice to free me from it.

"That was when an elderly musician slit his wrists and died at one of the angel's concerts."

Why had the musician chosen that place to die?

Had he also despaired when faced with true talent? Or had he wished to be enveloped in something beautiful in his last moments? There was no way to know that now.

But that incident started something, and there was a succession of people who killed themselves while listening to the angel's album of hymns. The angel's concerts were suspended, and he put a stop to sales of the CD.

Trembling, Mr. Mariya told us that the angel had removed himself from public view when that happened.

I watched him with a burrowing pain in my chest.

"The people who dream of being artists…they're all very cowardly and have no confidence and are easy to influence."

"While they're praised for their talent, they're up against a wall, and it's hard, so hard, and there's no options left for them…Even so, I've seen a fair number of people who can't give up, and their hearts grow sick."

He'd been talking about himself—!

Shaking visibly, Mr. Mariya took off his watch. There was the mark of a blade there.

Mr. Mariya had also attempted suicide while he listened to the angel's hymns. But he hadn't finished the job. He threw away the life he'd lived up to that point, and without telling anyone, he went on a trip.

"I wanted to forget about the angel. But no matter how far I went from Paris, that glistening voice echoed in my ears and wouldn't leave me. That voice pursued me everywhere. Ever since I first heard his voice, I was cursed. That had been no angel. It was the voice of a Phantom leading people to their destruction. When I returned to Japan finally—finally I thought I'd stopped hearing that song, but—"

Bent forward, gripping his head, Mr. Mariya muttered in a frail voice, "When we started seeing each other, Yuka was a kind, cheerful, average girl. She wanted to be an opera singer, but she stagnated, and she would always sing despite her confusion. I loved her all the more because, like me, she wasn't any kind of genius, just an ordinary person.

"But then Yuka met the angel and she changed. She believed what the angel told her over me, and her singing changed.

"When I heard that singing, I shuddered and felt nauseous.

"Yuka's singing was exactly like the angel's.

"Why?! What had I done? Why was the angel following me? Would he keep taking the things that were important to me? I tried to separate Yuka from the angel. But *I wasn't in time—*"

Suddenly, Mito shouted in an agitated voice, "That's just an excuse!! It doesn't change the fact that you strangled me and then ran off without me! *You killed me! You killed me! You killed me!*"

179

Mr. Mariya covered his ears and shook his head. The cold voice repeated the curse that would continue into eternity.

"You killed me.

"You killed me.

"You killed me."

At that point, I got the impression that Miu had appeared there and was jabbing a finger at me, accusing me.

"You killed me, Konoha!"

A wild pain shot through my chest. I was swallowed up in a pitch-black whirlpool, and unable to withstand the crushing terror, I cried out.

"Stop, please! Mr. Mariya didn't mean to kill Mito. He just wanted a peaceful life with her. He's not really a bad person. He's a weak, ordinary human being like us—"

I wanted her to forgive him.

I didn't want her to drive him into a corner and attack him anymore.

My plea wasn't a defense of Mr. Mariya, but rather of myself.

I hadn't had the slightest intention of hurting Miu. I hadn't wanted to do anything to make Miu dislike me.

It wasn't as if I had committed a crime that deserved a punishment equivalent to having my limbs torn off while I was still alive—to be glared at with those cold eyes, to be ignored, to be pushed away with the words *"You wouldn't understand!"* Not because I'd wanted to!

Even as I felt a dizzying despair at my own weakness and deceit, it took all my energy to keep my senses.

Even though Kotobuki was right next to me!

Even though she was still pale and trembling!

How could I defend the person who had laid hands on her best friend for my own disgusting self-defense?! I was awful—awful!

Then Mr. Mariya moaned in a low voice.

"Don't speak for me. What do you know?"

I was silenced as if I'd been slapped in the face.

Mr. Mariya's cheeks colored with humiliation, and his eyes flared with hatred as he glared at me.

"I never had even the slightest desire for an average, uneventful life. It's only the surrender of the common man that makes them say there's nothing better than a peaceful life...But that's all you could imagine. How could a carefree high school student like you understand that regret, that misery?!"

The warm days we had spent together—Kotobuki, Mr. Mariya, and I—

The peaceful space—

The time that had been so important; the memories all crashed down loudly around me.

Mr. Mariya closing his eyes in a contented smile through a gentle cloud of cinnamon-scented steam.

His sweet words like smooth, sleepy chai.

"I wanted the time I spent at leisure with the person I loved to be more important than anything."

"So I can affirm that I have no regrets about my decision. So long as I have a cup of chai, life is wonderful, and an ordinary life beats anything else."

My heart emptied, and the strength fell away from my body.

Had all the things he'd said to me been lies? Were the ugly words he'd spat out what he believed?

Freedom that wouldn't be taken away by anything, say. I'd been captivated by his gentle smile...

"I didn't want to have the supporting role of the rich and good-hearted Raoul! I wanted to be the Phantom, bursting with talent, even if I was called a monster! If I could become the Phantom by hurting people or killing them, I would have done whatever I needed to! But even when I killed Yuka, I remained Raoul wearing the mask of the Phantom!"

Was this the truth?

Was this for real?

How painful. How ugly. How selfish.

How fragile love and trust were—!

With sorrowful eyes, Tohko declared, "Raoul isn't a supporting role.

"He's the main character in the story where he saves Christine by unceasingly and forthrightly loving her. *Phantom of the Opera* wouldn't work without Raoul. It's in Raoul's light that the Phantom's shadow first stands out."

"What twisted logic...! Who in the world cares about that well-bred idiot Raoul? He's just a paper-thin nobody who only looks good on the surface. Before a true genius, he's a pitiable sham that no one would look at twice!"

Despair and madness spewed from every pore of Mr. Mariya's body. His eyes gleamed like a beast's; he howled fiercely, groaned, writhed, then roared again.

"You don't understand! You don't understand how I feel! Nobody does!!"

"You would never understand, Konoha."

The vision of Miu, which had been haranguing me just moments earlier, merged with Mr. Mariya and spat out a shower of strident words.

"None of you understand the first thing about it! If Yuka hadn't sung like that—if she hadn't made me remember that voice, I might have been able to go on living, deceiving myself.

"The angel, the Phantom destroyed that! He took everything! I hate the Phantom! I'll never forgive him!!"

Mr. Mariya couldn't hear anyone else's voice now.

The words of the book girl didn't reach him, either.

He stabbed his finger at the masked boy and screamed, "*You* and that girl Yuka that you let into your confidence, you both need to die! You're the ones who should be cursed!"

His spiteful words painted the world in shadow.

Despair like a black whirlpool convulsed my heart and pounded against my brain.

He was right. I didn't understand. I didn't understand how Mr. Mariya felt or how Miu felt! I didn't! Not at all!

The advice Mr. Mariya had given me had been so precious to me, too. I'd wanted to be like him.

It really would have been better not to know the truth!

I watched as if in a dream as the masked boy lifted his torn sleeves in loose folds and pulled a knife out of the sheath wrapped around his leg with a practiced grip.

I didn't care who did it, as long as someone put an end to this story filled with despair as soon as possible...

Just then, Kotobuki slipped past me and walked toward Mr. Mariya.

Kotobuki held the bouquet of blue roses that had fallen to the floor resolutely in her arms.

Her eyebrows arched, she bit down on her lip, and swung the bouquet up over her head with an angry look on her face, and then struck Mr. Mariya squarely in the face.

Petals as blue as the ocean fluttered away, and the bouquet fell to the floor with a thump.

In its wake appeared the dazed, wide-eyed face of Mr. Mariya, a petal still stuck to his cheek.

Kotobuki balled both her hands into fists, planted her feet, and shook.

The corners of her eyes were filled with tears as she glared at Mr. Mariya, and her expression quickly faltered, overflowing with sadness alongside her tears.

Surprise dawned on Mr. Mariya's face.

"Y-Yuka cared about you...a *lot*. These roses are the flowers you chose for her birthday...and she said that's why she fell for you. She took pictures and texted them to me. Telling me they were roses her boyfriend had sent. She sent me tons...Didn't you care about her?!"

It wasn't hatred or anger or even a curse, it was the pure-hearted cry of someone who cared about her best friend.

Maybe she reminded Mr. Mariya that the blue roses were memories of happier times.

That hatred hadn't been the only thing he had felt for Mito, that there had been love before that.

Sadness slowly rose into Mr. Mariya's face.

The moment that the Phantom, who in his sorrow had tried to kill Raoul, saw that Christine was spilling tears for his sake, he was healed and, for the first time in his life, fulfilled.

The diva was supported by a selfless love, and her tears flowed also beneath the cold mask and mingled with the tears in the

Phantom's eyes to shake the soul of the man who had been such a terrifying monster.

Poor, unhappy Erik.

The words of the diva saved that one wretched man who had no name but Phantom.

In the same way, Kotobuki's tears may have touched the gentleness inside Mr. Mariya.

He crumpled slowly to the floor.

A silver ring rolled across the floor... *cling*.

Mr. Mariya caught his breath and stared at it.

The masked boy whispered in a detached, low voice that seemed to be fighting back emotion, "Yuka clung to that till the very end. She never let go of it..."

His fingertips trembling, Mr. Mariya picked the ring up.

Then from the pocket of his suit, he took out another—a second ring of the same design.

Mito had written ecstatically in a message about how they had exchanged matching rings on Christmas Eve.

How they had promised to always keep them on, but he got teased when he wore it at school and so he took it off his finger and hid it.

How before a date, he would quickly pull it out and slip it on his finger.

How much she liked hiding and watching him do that.

"And then when he's sad, he squeezes my hand tight to get through it."

"When I touch his hand and he loosens his grip just a little... I feel so sublime and indulgent, and I think, Wow, I love him so much."

185

Mr. Mariya looked at the two rings that lay in his palm with a frail gaze that threatened tears at any moment.

Then he squeezed them firmly in both hands.

He hung his head and wept. There was no one left now who would gently loosen his grip.

Mr. Mariya had finally realized what it was he'd lost.

The petals of the blue roses that signified the blessings of God were scattered all around him.

There could be no forgiveness for what he'd done.

Nor could he take back the words he'd spoken.

But seeing Mr. Mariya, his shoulders shaking, tears continuing to pour down his face, I could feel the dark lump in my chest quietly melting away.

Tohko and Shoko both had sad expressions on their faces as well.

As she wiped away her tears with the back of her hand, Kotobuki sobbed and whined like a puppy.

I was still wondering if I had any right to do the same, feeling as if my heart would tear open—but even so, I reached out and embraced Kotobuki.

We didn't notice when the angel disappeared.

I'm sorry I made you cry so much, Nanase.

And that it doesn't look like I'm gonna be able to keep my promise about Christmas...

I'm pretty sure this will be the last message I send you.

You used to say that all you ever did was let me help you, but that's not true.

You were always giving me reasons to be happy actually.

You were always an awkward, straight-talking girl who never told a lie. The girls in class always pushed you into the role of telling boys what they'd done wrong, and you always got the short end of the stick, but I really loved that about you.

Back then, you hated boys and you said boys hated you, but I was sure that eventually there would be a boy who would understand what was so wonderful about you.

So the winter of our second year in middle school, when you came to me all embarrassed, your face bright red, and you told me, "Teach me how to pluck my eyebrows," I was as happy for you as I would have been for myself.

Because you wanted to be more girlie for the guy you liked, and because I could help you be pretty.

You were always totally devoted to being in love. It was really fun encouraging you while you were happy or sad or confused or soul-searching about Inoue.

I always thought you were so cute. You're cute, Nanase. You're really cute, the cutest girl in the whole world.

I always hoped that your feelings would come across to Inoue soon.

I always talked about how I wanted to go on a double date with my boyfriend, you, and Inoue, remember? Whenever I did, you would blush. It was so cute. It's too bad our four-person date never became a reality, but I still believe and pray that your love will come true.

I'm sorry that I couldn't give Yuka back to you. But Yuka feels peaceful and happy now, and she's singing tons of songs that she loves, so don't worry about her.

I'll consider you my best friend forever, Nanase.

I'll hope for your happiness with all of my heart.
If you're ever sad, remember the magic spell I sent you.

You're cute, Nanase. Really cute. The cutest girl in the whoooole world.

Chapter 8—I'll Go, Then.

It was Monday, the start of the week. A little after closing time, I paid a visit to the library with Tohko.

The room was dyed in the desolate darkness of sunset.

The counter was empty, and there was no sign of anyone in the reading area, either. If I listened carefully, I could faintly hear the *clack-clack* of someone typing on a keyboard.

We tried heading for the computer corner on one side of the room.

There we found Omi, his cheek awash in the light of the setting sun, typing with ease.

His glasses were shining, and I couldn't really read his expression.

"Omi...," I called out softly. His hands paused over the keys, and he looked at me.

His face was very still and calm. It looked like he'd guessed that we would come see him.

"Where's Mito? You know, don't you?"

"Hold on for three minutes," Omi murmured in a low voice, and he started typing again.

At last, he pressed the enter key; then he shut off the computer, stood up, and took off his glasses.

"It's a little far. Do you mind?"

When we got off the train, I sent a text. We walked a long way from there, then arrived at an old factory standing in an abandoned field. Without turning around, Omi explained in a detached voice that the factory was locked up now and wasn't used anymore. I sent another text at that point.

The area was thick with weeds, but there was also a single Christmas tree as tall as we were, shining in the light of the moon.

"Where are you?!"
"Inside a Christmas tree. That's my home."

I remembered the conversation we'd had on the phone, and a creaking desolation spread through my heart.

When Omi came to a stop in front of the tree, he knelt down on the grass and flipped the switch on the power supply that had been tossed aside there with a *click*. The next moment, the stars, churches, and angel wings decorating the tree glimmered brightly.

"Mito is sleeping...under here," Tohko murmured, her voice tinged with sadness.

His head still bent, Omi answered in a croaking voice, "Yuka loved Christmas trees. She was so excited when I brought a tree here. Yuka put up all of these decorations."

Mito had always said that she wanted to live in a Christmas tree, and in the end, I suppose Omi had granted her wish.

As he related the story with some detachment, his voice was different from the low, muffled voice he had at school or the overpowering high notes I'd heard in the music hall or the noble girl's voice from when we had talked on the phone; it was a strange, androgynous voice, nearly a woman's alto.

Just how many voices did he have?

The night before, I'd used my family's computer to look up the young man who had long ago been called an "angel" in Paris.

The young Asian man whose age, birthplace, professional background, and everything else were swathed in mystery had, some years earlier, been scouted while singing with a church's choir, and he became instantly popular.

Everyone lauded and idolized him as an angel who delivered people to the heavenly paradise and for the hymns he could perform in his shining voice that burst with a holy sound.

Even after his voice changed, audiences were simply astounded at the high clarity of his voice, and there were even those who suggested that the angel was probably a woman in men's clothing.

The sexless angel—

Eventually, that's what people started to call him.

The one Maki had been telling me about wasn't Mr. Mariya; it was Omi. I was sure she'd deliberately said it in a confusing way. Maki had said that occasionally the art world gave rise to unprecedented monsters. The angel had certainly been that.

Those who are men but nevertheless naturally possess a woman's register in their singing are called sopranists; male singers who produce a woman's register using a falsetto are called countertenors; and male singers who undergo castration in order to preserve the soprano of youth are called castrati.

There was no way to know which of these the angel was.

But he had given voice to a song of miracle before us all and had even pulled off an imitation of Mito's voice.

Afterward, Kotobuki had said that if she listened closely, she could tell it was different from Mito's voice.

She thought he had been adept at grasping the speed of her speech and miniscule habits and that with the mood of the place he had made her believe that Mito herself was talking.

I was convinced the many high voices I'd heard in the alley must have been a trick of his.

After a year of glorious activity, his concerts led to suicides and the angel abruptly disappeared from public view.

The angel's songs were songs of destruction that led people to their deaths—as that negative reputation spread, the angel's name was corrupted.

There were a great many people who wanted to hear his singing even so, but the angel never ventured to the stage. There were also people who said he really had been a girl after all, people who said he'd been kidnapped by a crazed fan, and people who said that puberty had stolen his clear voice.

Even now, years later, the truth hadn't come to light.

Standing in front of us now, looking at the Christmas tree with a friendless gaze, he was unrecognizable as the ordinary first-year high school boy who hid his face behind glasses, exuding an aura of illusion.

I wondered how old he really was... His bowed head was unusually handsome in profile, and he looked like he could be a boy or a girl, an adult or a child.

A creature who had surpassed time, sexless and pure—yes, exactly like an angel...

"I always had lessons with Yuka here," Omi told us, his voice hard, severe, and restrained. "I had no intention of getting involved at first..."

He gave a soft tsk, as if he was annoyed at himself.

The night they met, one of the heels had broken off Yuka's sandals and her clothes were ripped. Her right cheek was red and swollen, but through her tears she was singing.

Apparently she'd gotten a bad customer and been thrown out of his car.

She was singing a bright, happy song to keep herself from being swallowed up by sadness. And though she couldn't hold it back completely and her voice hitched and she wiped away the tears that spilled down her cheek again and again with the back of her hand, she continued to sing. At first, Omi watched this girl from hiding. But since her singing never stopped, he couldn't help calling out to her.

"You shouldn't sing like that. You'll ruin your voice."

The summertime, thick with the scent of grass.

He said that catching sight of him, appearing so suddenly, illuminated by the moonlight, had filled Mito's face with a terrible shock.

She had listened raptly, her eyes wide, when he picked up the song she'd dropped.

Then she had started singing, joining her voice to his.

Their duet went on for quite a while, Omi giving her brief, sporadic words of advice. Mito's voice gradually improved, as if pulled along in his wake, and a shining smile spread across her whole face.

He'd enjoyed himself, too.

He had closed off the option of singing in front of people, and it had been such a long time since he'd sung alongside the voice of another. His voice overlapping with someone else's and melting into one was enjoyable and made him happy, and he'd been in the mood to sing forever.

When morning came, he prepared clothes for Mito and then left without telling her his name or making any promises.

He had no intentions of interacting with anyone and he didn't want to have any expectations whatsoever.

Still Mito came to him the next night, and the night after that, and the night after that, and asked to take lessons from him.

When he wouldn't tell her his name, she laughed and said, "Then I'll just call you my angel, and it'll be fine. Like the Angel of Music in *Phantom of the Opera*. If you don't like that, you have to tell me your name."

Since he remained stubborn and wouldn't give his name, angel became his name.

Even though it should have been torture for her to call him that, when Mito called him "angel" with her clear voice, he felt good.

Mito wore him down and took instruction from him, and her voice changed with each passing day. Rather than improving in terms of technique, perhaps the fact that her spirit was liberated had a greater effect.

When she was singing, Mito always seemed to be energetic and to be enjoying herself.

Mito told him about a lot of things.

About her best friend Kotobuki, about her lover Mr. Mariya, about what books she liked, about her dreams for the future—and not just fun things but also painful things. She revealed everything to him. *"Maybe I've lost my way like Camellia. Maybe I'll lose everything someday, like Violetta,"* she whispered morosely. *"But there's nothing I can do about it. Debt collectors came to our house every day, and my dad can't be at his company anymore, and we wanted my little brother to go to high school. I can only do what I can... So yeah, there's nothing I can do about it. Right now I'm happy just being able to sing,"* she said and laughed.

"It hurts me to lie to Keiichi and Nanase, but I still want to believe that in the light of day, I'm the way I used to be, that nothing

has changed, that what happens at night is all a bad dream and the me when I'm awake is the real one."

When she said that, her face suddenly turned sad. *"But lately,"* she murmured, *"there have been times I think the way I am at night is the real me and the way I am in the daytime might be the illusion."*

"I'm a human being who gave up singing, but... Yuka truly loved songs. She was a great girl and talented, so I didn't want her to live like I had, concealed in the shadows, living in hiding from people. I wanted her to succeed somewhere the sun shone."

Staring at the faint lights burning on the Christmas tree, quietly relating his memories of being with Mito, Omi's face and voice were both colored by the sorrow and the solitude of a person who had lost something important to him.

Omi had been alone for a long time, so in his mind, Mito might have been someone who brought him light and warmth.

Like a single tiny Christmas tree glinting in the darkness.

Mito had been Omi's hopes, hadn't she?

What had the time they'd spent together here been like? What had they talked about? When I thought about that, my heart trembled uncontrollably, my throat and eyelids grew hot and burned painfully.

Tohko was probably having the same thoughts as me. Her eyes glistened with tears, and her lips were pursed sadly.

The event that had triggered Mito's weirdly intense obsession with songs had been learning of the deaths of her family. In order to try and forget the grievous cruelty of reality, Mito sang, and at the same time, she began to fiercely pursue success.

She threatened the assistant director Tsutsumi, seized the lead role in the recital, and spent night and day rehearsing. In playing Turandot, who attempts to avenge an ancestral princess, Mito seemed to be crying out against the world that had dealt her such suffering. It had made Omi uneasy.

In the midst of all that, tragedy happened.

"...Yuka was ragged when she appeared here that night. The marks of his hands around her neck stood out purple, and she had a head injury, too. Yuka said nothing except that she'd had a problem with a customer, and at first she seemed upbeat. But she gradually began to act strangely...and the next morning, she had breathed her last."

Tohko gazed at Omi, her look doleful, and she murmured, "So you sent tickets to each of Mito's clients under the name Camellia. You would draw the culprit there."

"...Even if I hadn't, seeing how Yuka was acting...I had already guessed who it was."

Omi's voice was hoarse, and he balled his hands into tight fists, as if to withstand the pain.

"Because if Yuka was covering for someone, he was the only one who came to mind..."

Seeing Omi bite down on his lip and stare fixedly into space, I felt my heart rending.

Omi, who had hidden Mito's corpse beneath the Christmas tree, had begun closely investigating Mr. Mariya. While he watched Mr. Mariya's movements, he must have turned away the doubts that surfaced again and again. Must have prayed desperately that by some chance someone else was the culprit.

More than anything, he must not have wanted to believe, for Mito's sake, that Mr. Mariya was the killer.

But his wish was not granted.

Mito had been killed at the hands of the person she loved best, and she had died protecting her lover.

"Even after Yuka died, her ring wouldn't come off, so I cut off her hand and forced the ring off. For my promise of revenge..."

197

It looked like Omi was holding back desperately so as not to let his emotions show.

In a kind voice, Tohko asked, "You kept sending Nanase messages from Mito's phone because you didn't want Nanase to worry, right?"

Omi turned his face away, as if to keep us from seeing it.

"If Nanase went by Yuka's house because she suddenly stopped hearing from her, it would have caused problems..."

Behind us there was the rustling sound of a step in the grass.

It was probably Kotobuki. She must have seen the messages I'd sent. I had said that we were far from the station, so she should take a cab.

Kotobuki had been out of school today with a fever. When I called her at lunch, she had apologized. Her fever had gone down, so she would be at school tomorrow, she said.

When I turned slightly, I saw Kotobuki standing in the shadow of the building, her cheeks flushed and out of breath, on the verge of tears.

Omi continued his story, unaware of her.

"If Nanase hadn't walked over to Mariya that day—if Mariya hadn't spilled his tears when he saw Yuka's ring—I would have cut his throat. I know Yuka wouldn't have wanted that, but I would have done it. Nanase...stopped me."

With a searing pain, I recalled once again the dark despair of that day, the implacable sense that we were all trapped.

Two eternally parallel lines that would never reach an understanding.

Stones inside words clashing simply to hurt each other.

Kotobuki's straightforward concern had been what overturned that state of despair.

"...Don't get Nanase involved. "
"She's the only thing you need to keep your eyes on, Inoue."

Omi bit down on his lip and hung his head.

He had probably also wanted to protect the friend that Mito held so dear.

Calling me on the phone pretending to be Mito and coming down so hard on me were also because he was worried about Kotobuki...I'm sure I looked unreliable, and he'd gotten annoyed.

Omi lifted his eyes awkwardly and looked at me with a clumsily hard gaze.

"...I was wrong to call you a hypocrite. Thank you for being there to support Nanase."

My heart fluttered at those words.

"She's the one who supported me actually."

His tense eyes became a little timid, and a sad-looking shadow crossed them.

I realized what he'd just said was probably a good-bye, and I started.

"What will you do now?"

Omi's face grew suddenly harsh again, and he turned his eyes away.

"I'll go somewhere else. I've always traveled up till now."

"What about school?"

"I'll quit. I was only there as part of a 'contract.' And that's over."

"A contract...with Maki?" Tohko asked.

"I can't answer that," he answered resolutely.

I felt like he was giving up on a lot of things and was despairing, and my heart squeezed tight, so I said, "Why do you have to go? Can't you stay here? You're free, aren't you? So can't you keep living here the way you have been?"

"It won't do any good...Even now, my foster parents are looking everywhere for me. They were my managers. They probably still think I have some commercial value. It's too dangerous to stay in one place for long."

"So you're going to live in hiding forever? You're never going to sing for people again?"

I gazed at the boy's desolate profile, illuminated faintly by the light of the Christmas tree, and felt like crying.

He was like me.

A boy with the voice of a girl who, in the midst of brilliant admiration, disappeared suddenly from the public eye.

Myself, a novelist who had the name of a girl and quit writing after publishing one best seller.

It was like I was looking at myself, and I felt empty.

Omi raised his face and looked at me with darkly sorrowful eyes.

"Do you think Miu Inoue will write another book?"

It was like I'd been stabbed in the heart.

I would never write another novel.

An author was the one thing I would absolutely never be.

Two years earlier, I'd made that tearful vow.

I didn't know how Omi knew my secret. Maybe he'd investigated me, too.

But maybe you feel it, too—the sympathy I have in my heart.

That we resemble each other.

And in fact, maybe that's why he asked whether Miu would write another book.

I was sure he understood that I couldn't answer.

And he probably wanted to convey that that was his answer.

The angel would never sing again.

"Singing didn't make me happy."

My heart broke at those sadly whispered words.

Novels had brought me nothing but disaster. I was tortured by that false version of myself, and I'd lost Miu. I had thought Miu Inoue was a beautiful name—but at some point it was disgustingly corrupted and became a name that gave me nothing but pain and remorse.

Sadness spread through the depths of my heart like ripples across the surface of a river.

With a self-deprecating smile on his lips, Omi said, "Mariya said that he wanted to be the Phantom, even if it meant being a monster. But I always wanted to be Raoul."

I could tell that was his heartfelt wish.

The Phantom says it in *Phantom of the Opera*, too. That he's tired of doing things normal people don't do.

"Now I want to live like everybody else."

"I want to have a wife like everybody else and to take her out on Sundays."

"I have invented a mask that makes me look like anybody. People will not even turn around in the streets."

Below the vibrant opera house, he built his own kingdom, and while he sang, played piano, and composed music there, the disfigured Phantom dreamed of living in the sunlit world without having to justify himself.

No one called him by his true name in the solitary darkness.

Tohko had said that I needed to read the story to the end.

Because if I didn't, I wouldn't know the truth about the story.

Just then, Tohko, who had been sadly silent, opened her mouth.

"Yes. I think so, too. Being Raoul would be such a happy, wonderful thing."

Omi gazed at Tohko.

Tohko looked back at him, her eyes clear. The wind had begun to blow, and her long braids swayed in it slightly.

"*Phantom of the Opera* is a cruel fairy tale. A man who hides his disfigured face under a mask falls in love with a girl in unhappy circumstances, and she transforms into a princess through his magic. But the one she loved was a handsome young prince.

"Christine would never choose the Phantom.

"Even though he was a person who 'would have been one of the most distinguished of mankind' if only he weren't disfigured—even though he's a person she could sympathize with who hid his amazing talent—in the end Christine chooses Raoul."

Her sorrowful voice scattered in the cold wind.

Omi listened to Tohko's words with an expression of pain.

"*Phantom of the Opera* is that kind of story.

"But that's exactly why this story spills over with sadness and is so beautiful.

"The gothic novel painted up in darkly decadent beauty transforms at the very, very end into a candid tale that makes your heart tremble through the truth the Phantom shows us—

"It's like a thick, rich foie gras that sticks to your tongue being washed away, purified, and elevated in an instant by a dainty glass filled with chilled Perrier."

The faint light of the moon shone palely on Tohko's slender body and her small face.

Why did Tohko's eyes look so sad?

Her face was determined, her eyes drooping, as if she were speaking to a phantom that was about to disappear.

"*Phantom of the Opera* wasn't as well received as *Mystery of the Yellow Room*, another of Leroux's works, which is called a closed-room mystery. They said that as a mystery novel, it was preposterous and full of faults, and as a work of fine literature, it was too lowbrow.

"But in this story, Leroux created an unforgettable character in the Phantom.

"When they finish reading the story, a lot of people are struck by the Phantom's sorrow, and they can't help but wonder what the path he traveled must have been like, relying on the clues offered in the story. And they hope he'll be saved, whatever form it may take. When you finish reading the story, you feel like the Phantom is a real person.

"Christine wouldn't choose him.

"But the reader won't forget him.

"They won't forget the Phantom's lamentations, his life, his love.

"They love the disfigured Phantom who casts off his mask."

Speaking with dewy eyes, maybe Tohko wanted to give something to Omi, who had lost everything and was on the verge of leaving.

Words that would be like a tiny light to warm his heart when he grew sad and alone in the future—

The best she could do, with all her heart, as long as time would allow was—

"You know, a lot of people really have loved the Phantom when they read *Phantom of the Opera*! There have been more movies and plays and other interpretations of this book than you could count! There have been so many studies of the Phantom, and there are even blond youths who wear no masks as Phantoms.

"The British author Frederick Forsyth, who's famous for writing *The Day of the Jackal*, wrote about what happens to the Phantom afterward in *The Phantom of Manhattan*, in which he moves to America, and the author Susan Kay vividly, and with sensitive love and a fertile imagination, described the Phantom's background and the reasons that led to him living in the opera house, which had only barely been alluded to in the original. Her book *Phantom* is a masterpiece you absolutely ought to read.

"The character of the Phantom who was born from a single book has found new life and spread around the world and is giving birth to new readers, to imagination, and to different stories. People's imaginations have given new life to the Phantom.

"That's how much the Phantom is loved, and he'll continue to be loved. That's how much charm the Phantom and this story have. But y'know—"

Tohko squeezed her hands into fists, her eyes drooped, and she shouted with power, "If you don't read *Phantom of the Opera* to the very end, you wouldn't know that!"

Omi's eyes widened at Tohko's energy.

The wind rustled the grass and trees.

Tohko's face was tense and on the verge of tears. Her clear voice flared like quiet, sorrowful music.

"I love books, and I've gotten a lot of happiness, been comforted, been healed when I read them.

"I'll read any story to the very end to get a true taste of it. But sometimes I wonder, what would happen if this story suddenly ended right here?

"What if the author had quit writing?

"When I think about that, I feel sad and stung, and I feel a pressure on my chest.

"If Gaston Leroux had ended *Phantom of the Opera* partway

through, the Phantom would have remained an ugly monster. Neither Raoul nor Christine would have been saved."

She looked straight up at Omi, who was wavering still, with her black, wet eyes; then Tohko murmured as if in prayer, "Keep on writing your story.

"Let the people who are waiting to hear you sing read it."

Omi gulped.

Full of fire, her voice earnest, Tohko appealed to him, "Maybe singing didn't make you happy. But there are a huge number of people who felt happy when they heard your songs. Otherwise you wouldn't be an 'angel.' Just like the Phantom is loved by readers, you're loved by your audience. You just don't realize it—*no, you cover your ears and don't try to realize it.*"

I saw a violent shock run over Omi's face.

"It's not that guys like you don't notice. You just don't want to know."

Those words had now come flying back at him.

"Your singing has the power to make people happy. I know that your singing saved Mito, too."

"You're wrong!!"

Omi had been standing frozen in a daze, but now his face twisted and he shouted, as if lashing out at her.

"Yuka didn't get saved! If she hadn't met me—if I hadn't taught her to sing—she would have gotten through this without Mariya hating her or killing her!"

His eyes were crazed. His fists were balled up tightly, his cheeks were ruddy, and his lips trembled as if the emotions he'd been desperately fighting down all that time had exploded.

"That Mariya had heard the angel sing in Paris, that he held such a grudge against the angel—that he'd been driven so far that he cut his wrists—I didn't know that! That Yuka's voice had mine—that it had overlapped with the angel's voice!!—it's like I destroyed her!"

The pain and suffering and remorse he was feeling stabbed into my heart.

His scream was one of such anguish, his voice so sad.

When Mr. Mariya had spat out his words of hatred for the angel, this was how hurt, how filled with despair Omi had been beneath his mask!

Tohko appealed to him in a majestic voice.

"I understand that you feel responsible for Mito's death and that you're sad. But don't deceive yourself. When she met you, Mito was working as Camellia, cutting her heart to ribbons. It's not your fault Mito died. Far from it. By encountering your singing, Mito found some comfort in her painful life."

Omi shook his head violently from side to side.

"No! No!! If I hadn't interfered, Yuka never would have died in that pitiful way! It's just like Mariya said. I confused Yuka and dragged her into my subterranean darkness. I'm sure that in her heart, Yuka reviled me."

"Really?!" Tohko asked, her face sternly set. "Did Mito truly revile you? Don't you think you've just convinced yourself of that because you're a captive to your own guilty conscience?"

"It's not like that. I'm not—"

"Then talk about what happened when Mito died! What did you two talk about at the end?"

Omi bit down on his lip and fell into a pained silence. The memory alone was probably torture. He squeezed his eyes tightly shut. I felt my heart breaking, too.

Kotobuki tried to stay hidden in the shadow of the building, watching Omi. Her face was strained, too.

"...Please, tell us," Tohko said in a quiet yet intent tone that allowed him no escape.

Omi flinched, then opened his eyes a sliver, the pain apparently under control. He bit his lip several times, as if at a loss for how to begin; looked down at his feet; and then began to speak in a hoarse voice.

"...That night, Yuka was unusually keyed up...I told her she should rest because she was hurt, but she wouldn't listen and cheerfully declared that the recital was coming up so we had to have a lesson.

"She talked about how sure she was that they would put on an amazing performance...

"Yuka's voice held notes better than usual and seemed steady. She laughed that she was in the mood to sing until morning that day...Maybe Yuka was trying to forget about everything by singing, like the night I first met her...

"It really did seem like she would go on singing forever if I let her, so I forced her to take a break. We sat in a clump of grass, and as we were looking at the Christmas tree, Yuka said, 'Our tree really is adorable. It's great.' We were talking about nothing important, like that, when out of nowhere Yuka leaned on my shoulder and sweetly said, *"Keiichi? It'd be nice if we could have a fun Christmas Eve like we did last year."*

Omi's voice faltered, then broke off.

"Yuka—she was talking as if I were Mariya."

I gasped at the despondent confession.

"And? What happened next?" Tohko asked, her eyes unwavering.

"...Even though I realized Yuka was acting strangely, I couldn't do anything. Yuka seemed...so happy."

"Did you keep on talking to her as Mr. Mariya?"

"...Yuka did most of the talking. Saying they should have a

party at Keiichi's place for Christmas Eve, that she would take care of the food, asking what he wanted to eat. She apologized for not being able to see him so much...told him that she always wore her ring..."

My chest trembled at a wrenching pain.

How must he have felt, listening to Mito talk?

Helpless to do anything, how had he felt...?

After that, he said Mito had called Kotobuki's house on her cell phone. When Kotobuki spoke with Mito for the last time, it hadn't been Mr. Mariya holding her Mito in his arms; it had been Omi.

"I'm with my boyfriend right now. The Christmas tree is so pretty, and he's holding me in his arms, so I'm all toasty warm. Hey, Nanase, you've gotta hurry up and get a boyfriend. Then let's all go out on a double date. It'll be so fun."

Kotobuki's eyes screwed shut to fight down a sob, and she bit down on her lip.

Omi turned his face away so we wouldn't see his expression.

"And then?"

Tohko gently urged him on.

"...Ngh. She hung up and said, *'Nanase's so cute...I hope her love works out...Nanase's—'...*Ngh, *'Nanase's—'* she said, *'I hope she'll be happy like in Miu Inoue's book...'"*

My heart thudded loudly.

Happy like in Miu Inoue's book—!

Mito had said that?!

Omi kept saying one thing after another about Miu Inoue. That Mito recommended the book to Mr. Mariya. That Miu's book was gentle, innocent, unassuming, precious, and gave her relief. That Itsuki and Hatori were cute and she loved them—

"Promise me now. Read Miu. She's my favorite author. While I'm reading her book, I can forget that painful things happen."

I had never before thought that there were people who felt something after reading my book.

That someone I'd never seen, someone I didn't know, liked my book.

My brain burned, and feelings I couldn't describe welled up to fill my throat.

Kotobuki covered her face with both hands, crouched down on a tuft of grass, and her shoulders trembled.

In a voice as clear as the moonlight, Tohko asked, "And then? What did you do?"

Omi was shaking, too. His head bent, biting his lip, he forced the words out.

"'Sing a hymn,' Yuka told me. 'I want to hear one now, more than anything…Please, I want you to sing…' Her eyes were so clear…So…so I—"

"So you sang for her," she whispered gently. "You did a *wonderful* thing for her."

Omi's face twisted sourly.

"I was never going to sing again! Because so many people died when they heard me sing hymns! So I was never, ever going to sing again—but I felt like I would never see Yuka again, I felt like it was her last wish—and I sang! Yuka's eyes stayed closed and she stopped moving. The next morning, her heart had stopped! She didn't open her eyes, no matter how much I called to her!

"Yuka died because I sang!"

"You're wrong!" Tohko shouted fiercely. "Think back! What did Mito's face look like as she listened to you sing?!"

Omi shook his head.

"Remember it! Remember Mito's eyes, her lips, her breathing—remember what they were telling you in her final moments!"

Tohko wouldn't stop hurling questions at him. Omi had his ears covered, but her long braids swinging, illuminated by the moonlight, fiercely, wildly—she was exactly like the ghosts in *A Christmas Carol* who appear to the moneylender Ebenezer Scrooge on Christmas Eve, trying to break apart the armor that covered his heart and drag out the truth.

"Go on, tell us the story you witnessed for Mito! Don't be the one to sully the memories you have of her!"

His head still bent, Omi brought his hands tightly together. The truth he had seen ... It was about to be revealed from his very lips.

"—Yuka leaned on my chest and clutched her ring in her hand ... and she closed her eyes ... and she was smiling! The whole time I was singing ... ! Then she said ... '*Oh, how beautiful ... Keiichi*' ... Ngh, she said, '*It's like a real angel singing*' ... And then—"

His voice caught and he was racked by a sob.

A small voice like a whisper related Mito's last words.

"She said ... '*I'm so happy*.'"

That same instant, huge tears rolled from Omi's eyes and fell down his cheek. He pressed his clasped hands to his mouth, and keeping his face down, he wept violently, like a child.

"I'm so happy."

Mito had said that, smiled, and then passed away.

Enveloped in the singing of an angel, her eyes closed, and in tranquil joy.

211

"That's the truth about Mito."

The book girl softly gave him the words that transformed the cruelly long tale at the last moment into a tale of a prayer, filled with pure, gentle light.

Kotobuki stood up and ran over to him.

She grabbed Omi's hands and lifted them, covering them in both of her own, and Omi looked up in surprise.

His teary eyes opened wide, and Kotobuki looked back at him with her own reddened eyes.

Then she placed a kiss atop his clasped hands.

Like Christine, who kissed the Phantom's forehead—

"Thank you for your kindness to Yuka."

Seeing Kotobuki do her very best to smile with a face that was streaked and puffy from crying, tears fell once again from Omi's eyes. He gazed at Kotobuki with a frail look and drew his face to her ear.

He appeared to whisper something to her.

Kotobuki started, and then her face quickly threatened tears again.

He slipped away from her, rubbed roughly at his tears with his arm and the back of his hand; then Omi's face set into a fearless expression, as if everything had been wiped away, and he started walking.

I tried to stop him as he slipped past me, but he murmured in a soft voice, "Take care of Nanase."

Then he left Kotobuki, who was trembling, her eyes filled with tears; left me, standing rooted as my heart practically ripped in half; left Tohko, who watched him go with clear eyes that seemed to pray for him; and without ever turning back, he disappeared into the darkness.

That was the last we ever saw of the angel.

Epilogue—To You, My Dear Friend

In the end, I couldn't tell him that I didn't hate Miu Inoue. Maybe that was because I was jealous of him.

That day Yuka died, a call came from Nanase on Yuka's phone. I listened to her panicked voice on the voice mail saying, "Mori and the others told Inoue that I like him. What'm I gonna do?" after I'd buried Yuka's body beneath the Christmas tree.

I didn't want to tell Nanase that Yuka was dead, wanted to protect Nanase's life at least, and I returned her message as Yuka.

I wonder when it was that I became aware of the Nanase that Yuka talked about almost every night.

Nanase was in love with Konoha Inoue, a boy in her grade, and she frequently asked for Yuka's advice.

"I got nervous standing in front of Inoue and accidentally glared at him"; or "He must think I'm an awful person. It's over. What am I gonna do?"; or "I managed to talk to him a little today, so that was really nice"; or "I'm thinking of baking cookies, but I don't know what flavors boys like"; or "I'll just try cutting back on the sugar overall..." They were minor things, and Yuka would always have fun talking to me about Nanase's awkwardness.

About how in middle school, Nanase regularly went to a library to see Inoue or how she'd hated boys until then, but she suddenly started acting like a girl and practiced drawing in her eyebrows with real dedication—

"Nanase really is adorable, y'know. I hope her love comes true."

She would always say that at the end in a kind, dreamy tone of voice.

Around that time, I was enrolled at Seijoh Academy and I was helping in the library just like Nanase, so I was able to observe her behavior up close.

The real Nanase was even more beautiful than in her pictures, but she was a girl who pursed her lips and pouted, and at first glance she looked harsh.

But I knew that was only bravado, so the childish blushing she let out when her guard fell or when she got frantic made my lips start to stretch into a smile despite myself, and it got me in trouble. I see. Yuka's right. There's no other girl as genuine as Nanase.

I went to peek into their class to see about Konoha Inoue, too, to confirm it. I thought he had a girlie face and seemed unreliable, and the reason I got such a bad impression of him from the very start was probably because I was annoyed at his idiocy for not noticing how Nanase felt. His indecisiveness rubbed me the wrong way, and I deliberately said mean things to him, and even lured him down an alley and used my voices to intimidate him.

Inoue's last girlfriend was always on Nanase's mind.

Nanase said she'd gotten an e-mail from her. Apparently she wrote some pretty awful stuff, like that Konoha was her dog and Nanase shouldn't go anywhere near him and that if she tried to steal what belonged to someone else she'd be cursed. And Nanase, who was already vulnerable because of what was going on with Yuka, was utterly beaten.

Nanase sent a tearful message to Yuka's phone saying that she'd gotten a text from the Phantom and asked her to help by please, please coming home.

Still I couldn't do anything for Nanase, who was hurt and afraid.

Even when she fled her house at the shock of learning that Yuka's entire family had committed suicide, all I could do was watch from outside the window, feeling my heart ripping apart as Nanase buried her face in her knees and cried alone in Yuka's house.

The one who came to Nanase and comforted her was not me, but Konoha Inoue.

That was probably for the best.

Even if when Inoue held Nanase in his arms, when she clung to him as she cried, when Nanase's lips finally confessed the feelings she'd kept locked away, the breath was knocked out of me and I felt like I'd been cast into a fire.

Nanase's happiness was Yuka's hope and my greatest wish.

Konoha Inoue wasn't an average boy like he seemed at first sight.

There was a deep sludge of darkness in his heart.

While I was investigating the girl who sent Nanase the

threatening messages, I learned Inoue's secret. Maybe something happened between Inoue and the girl—

That was when I thought, maybe Konoha Inoue and I are like a hall of mirrors. Something similar while still being different in every way. But still similar—

Maybe that was why I couldn't totally ignore him despite my annoyance.

I didn't really hate Miu Inoue, either.

I felt loathing for her too-pretty world but also longing.

I don't think that Inoue's last girlfriend will stay quiet for long.

And then there's Inoue's upperclassman, Tohko Amano. She's the closest one to Inoue, but her interior is wrapped up in mystery, and I couldn't read her. Not just anyone can make *me* cry.

How does Amano feel about Inoue? That book girl could by some chance turn out to be the most threatening Phantom for Nanase.

But in the end, Nanase will probably claim victory.

Inoue is beginning to lean toward her.

He's beginning to notice Nanase's kindness, her determination, her strength, her love, and to be drawn to it.

Nanase could never become a Phantom. But she could become a Raoul.

The rest depends on how hard Nanase tries.

Keiichi Mariya and Shoko Kagami both turned themselves in to the police, and my revenge is complete.

I've finished my 'contract,' too, and said my good-byes, and all that remains is to leave for new soil.

This place was the castle of darkness I made so that Yuka

could release her feelings. I put many layers of protection on it, devised many traps, and made it so that no one but Yuka and I could access it.

After Yuka died and I decided to take revenge on her behalf, I continued to update it in her stead. I hit the keys with Yuka's feelings and wrote the text as Yuka. In so doing, perhaps I let out my own feelings.

The guilt I felt toward Yuka, my concern for Nanase...

I'll probably never come here again, but I think I'll leave this page exactly the way it is.

In the photo that fills the entire screen, Yuka and Nanase are both smiling happily. I'm making a slightly embarrassed face.

Some day, by some chance, I hope someone runs across this website, and when they've read Yuka's words and seen the pictures, I hope they understand her a little bit.

And adorable Nanase.

As I whispered into your ear at the end, I hope from the bottom of my heart that your love comes true.

———◈———

I celebrated the twenty-fourth, Christmas Eve, at a restaurant Ryuto went to all the time.

We'd rented out the country-themed restaurant, which looked like it could have been in a Western—I'd been there before—and put up flashy red and gold Christmas decorations.

"I actually wanted you two alone on a date, y'know," Ryuto griped beside me.

"I'd get assassinated by a girl if I did that."

In every part of the restaurant, flashy girls were looking hard at each other, feinting at one another. It may have been a stimulat-

217

ing environment for Ryuto, who loved a good massacre, but for me it was pretty distasteful.

"Hey, not with me...Geez, why does this keep happenin'?"

Ryuto's eyes rolled away in a bitter look. There stood Tohko, dressed like Santa Claus in a red jacket and miniskirt with white fur trim and a red pointed hat. She pulled presents out of a big sack that was slung over her shoulder and handed them out to everyone.

At first she sounded embarrassed—"Why do I have to dress like this? Ugh, this skirt is so short"—but then she got completely into it, and she tossed people smiles along with their gifts.

"Geez, Tohko! I told ya this wasn't the time to be doin' that."

"You're right. She's got her National Center Test next month. She's got no awareness of the fact that she's got exams."

"S'not what I meant."

Ryuto groaned just as a petite girl with fluffy clouds of hair approached.

"Helloooo, Konohaaa."

"Oh, Takeda's here, too."

"Yup! Tohko invited meee," Takeda answered grinning. She was wearing a yellow mohair sweater with a gray skirt. "'Cos I'm between boyfriends right now, and I was gonna have a looonely Christmas Eve. I was totally lucky."

"What's this now? Izzat true? A cutie like you? How 'bout me, then? 'Cos I'm lookin' for a girlfriend, too."

"Wow, how cool! Are you Konoha's friend? My name's Chia Takeda. I'm a first-year at Seijoh Academy."

"Hey, same as me. I'm Ryuto Sakurai. Me and Konoha are real close, and I'm like family to Tohko."

"Whoooa, you're a *first*-year? I thought you were in college!"

"Ryuto! If you add any more girlfriends, you really will get stabbed!" I commented pointedly, but Ryuto gave me a relaxed smile.

"Oh, I'm a veteran. I'm used to it."

"Wooow, that's *awe*some!"

Takeda applauded wildly. This was bad.

"Which reminds me, is Akutagawa or anybody coming, too?"

"Akutagawa said he had other plans. He could be spending tonight with a girlfriend..."

"Ohhh, does Akutagawa have a girlfriend?"

"No, I just... thought that might be it. Oh, Kotobuki is coming. Maki said she would just make an appearance."

Tohko had shouted, *"You're not invited! Don't come!"* but Maki had put on an eerie smile and said, *"Of course, I'm going. To see the costume I gave you."* The miniskirt Santa outfit was the "compensation" for information—or rather, the "interest."

Maki appeared, bathing in the stares of the entire restaurant.

She had a fur shawl wrapped over a trailing dress with a deeply plunging neckline. A diamond necklace glittered brilliantly at her throat. She was dressed like she had snuck out of some celebrity's party somewhere. To put it plainly, she stuck way, way out.

"Argh, Maki! I told you not to come!!"

Maki grinned slyly at Tohko's squawking and let her gaze rove over Tohko's body.

"Yes, yes, it looks good on you, wonderful. This is what Christmas Eve is all about. If you would take off everything but that hat for me, it would be even more lovely and aesthetic, though."

"Ugh... you're so gross, Maki!"

Maki, whose eyes narrowed as she smiled, suggesting that she felt wonderful being insulted, made my spine shudder. This girl was seriously weird.

And on top of that, she never let her guard down...

The day after Omi left, Maki breezily revealed the details of his "contract."

She probably figured that it didn't matter since he wasn't around anymore. She had talked to Tohko and me in her workroom while she drank tea.

In order to help Mito, Omi had been collecting evidence of wrongdoing by the finance company who was collecting from Mito's father. He came to ask Maki to work the police and the media, saying, *"It should be possible for you, the scion of the Himekuras."*

In exchange, he was planted as a student at the school, and under orders from Maki, he gathered information and did investigations.

"There was one other condition I gave, and it was this."

She showed us a watercolor painting she had made of Omi, a white sheet over his head covering his bare skin, looking both feminine and masculine.

When she'd said "model," she had meant Omi!

"It's pretty good, right? Maybe I'll call it *Angel*."

The picture of the angel turning his cold gaze on the viewer felt totally transparent and solitary.

My heart ripped apart thinking about Omi, who'd lived such a long time alone, as I gazed at the painting with Tohko.

Perhaps because the Himekura family applied pressure, the fact that Mr. Mariya had committed murder didn't become a big story in the news. Sugino, who'd loved Mr. Mariya without any return in her feelings, fervently told me, her eyes bright red, as she was racked by sobs again and again, "When I was depressed because my friends were ignoring me, Marmar made me chai and comforted me. He was a good person really!"

"You're right, Mr. Mariya was a good person," I responded, recalling the sweet smell of chai, the gentle steam, the face of the man smiling through it, and my chest squeezed tight.

"What do you know?" he'd said.

That he'd never wanted an average, peaceful life.

But the time I'd spent with Mr. Mariya and Kotobuki, when I thought back on it, was something sweetly sad and warm after all. Mr. Mariya and Shoko had simply lost their way at some point. They weren't bad people—even if Mr. Mariya denied it, I wanted to believe that.

The financial company who'd been conducting unprincipled collections was under a major investigation, too, and it was almost a certainty that the upper levels would be arrested, and their business would be suspended.

The incidents involving the "angel" had ended.

After a round of teasing Tohko, Maki came over to Ryuto.

"Oh, you're still alive? I thought a girl might have cracked your skull open and stuffed you like a dead animal," she said sarcastically, smiling.

Ryuto smiled back at her, aggressively abrasive. "Well, I am a masochist. My only desire is for someone to love me that much."

Maki suddenly pulled Ryuto's face closer with both hands.

In fact, she stopped right next to Ryuto's lips, but to everyone else it had probably looked like she had kissed him. Screams went up all over, and the restaurant grew rowdy. Watching from one side, Takeda and I both widened our eyes, as well.

Ryuto gaped as Maki told him alluringly, "Then get killed a hundred times over."

She continued. "Grandpa and the rest of them are going to start complaining, so I'm going back to the estate. I'll see you."

Then she went away, wearing an invigorated expression.

"Hey now!" Ryuto wailed as all the girls surrounded him, looking murderous, and things started to get out of control. "Who was that?!" "Exactly how many girls are you gonna cheat on me with?" "You need to clear things up *today!* Who are you going home with later?!"

We quickly withdrew.

"It looks like Tohko's little brother really *is* going to get his head split open!"

"Takeda, it scares me when you say stuff like that with a smile on your face. Please don't do that."

"Heh-heh. I think it'd be scarier if I said it with a straight face, though."

As we were talking in this way, I spotted Kotobuki at the entrance.

She was wearing a billowing skirt and was glancing around nervously.

"Oh, I suddenly need to go to the bathroom. Why don't you go over to Nanase, Konoha?"

"Wha—? But, Takeda—"

"Don't you worry about me. I can get along with anyone, y'know."

After giving me a smile, her eyes grew suddenly knowing; then Takeda grinned guilelessly again and she left me.

Was this going to be all right?

When I went over to Kotobuki and called out to her, there was tension in my voice, but her face cleared in apparent relief.

"Inoue…"

"Hello. Did you see Tohko yet?"

"No, not yet. I'm a little late…I just got here."

"Okay. She's gonna be surprised. Takeda's here, too."

"Yeah, I heard."

"Do you want something to drink?"

"An orange juice, thanks..."

Kotobuki was still a little down. But she was trying hard to act cheerful. It was stilted, but she was smiling.

"Here you go."

"Thanks."

The two of us stood by the wall and talked.

Kotobuki and I were both being considerate...which made me recall that even when everything was over, the pain and sadness we'd felt that day hadn't disappeared from inside our hearts. Mito would never again come back to Kotobuki. Would Kotobuki spend Christmas alone...?

"Kotobuki—if you want, we could go somewhere together tomorrow. It's gonna be Christmas, though, so everywhere's probably going to be crowded."

Kotobuki shook her head.

"Thanks. But I promised Yuka I would keep the day open for her. I'm going to spend it reading a book she liked and eating cake."

A smile appeared on her lips, and she said quietly, "And...I'm thinking of trying out Miu Inoue."

The unflinching gaze she turned on me struck me as something extremely beautiful—and at the same time, I was made aware of my own weakness and grew embarrassed.

To hide these feelings, I smiled, too.

"Oh yeah? Then I'll just have a slow day at home, too."

"Oh, b-but—I'll send you a Christmas text. I...I'd like it if you sent me one back...okay?"

"Sure thing."

"Also..." Kotobuki was getting redder and redder, and she hung her head. "I can't do Christmas, but I'm free another day. So, um...if you invited me again, I...would really like that."

"Let's go somewhere during winter break, then."

When I said that, she raised her face, and her cheeks still flushed bright red, she smiled as openly as a child.

"Okay!"

"Take care of Nanase."

I felt as if I could hear his voice in my ears...

Maybe Omi really had wanted to be with Kotobuki and encourage her more than anything... When that thought occurred to me, my heart grew melancholy again.

I didn't know how much I was capable of doing, but I hoped I could be some help in cheering Kotobuki back up.

Kotobuki's curfew was ten o'clock, so after I took her home, I went to visit the factory where we'd parted ways with Omi.

Mito's body had been dug up, and she was resting in a grave with her family now. The Christmas tree was still there, and when I turned the switch on, the lights glittered brightly.

The snowflakes that shone with a pale light, the twinkling red and gold stars, the dolls that looked like they'd been made with cookie cutters, the house with a chimney, Santa Claus, the faceless angel—

The glass angel had two wings fixed to its triangular body, and there was nothing above its shoulders.

As I looked at it, I thought about a lot of things.

About Mr. Mariya who'd wanted to become the Phantom.

About Omi, who'd had no choice but to live as the Phantom.

And about Miu.

"Y'know, Konoha, if you wish for something on Christmas Eve, it'll come true. What do you want?"

"... Then promise when you become a writer, you'll give your first autograph to me."

"Geez, that again? I told you, it's way too soon for that."

Miu giggling and planting a lightning-quick kiss on my cheek. She'd caught me off guard, and my face was bright red as she bent slightly at the waist and then spoke with a teasing look.

"That ... was a promise."

When I touched the angel's wings, my fingertips twitched at the chill.

As I remembered that long ago Christmas with melancholy emotions that seemed to rankle deep in my heart, I whispered, "Miu...you know I've hated Miu Inoue this whole time. I thought her whole book was a bunch of lies and the stupid scribblings of a child.

"I hated Miu Inoue...more than anyone in the whole world.

"But...Mito said she liked Miu Inoue...

"That she thought back on Miu's book all the time, like it was a memory...That she loved both Itsuki and Hatori...that when she was reading Miu's book, she could forget all the painful things in her life...She talked to Omi about that..."

In the freezing cold, my throat drew tight and tears welled up in my eyes.

"I wonder where you are now, Miu. I wonder what you're feeling. I wonder if...you can forgive me for not rejecting Miu Inoue anymore..."

Miu Inoue's book was the story of the trivial days that Miu and I spent together.

Kotobuki had said that she'd been watching us the whole time. That when I was with Miu, I laughed happily.

225

"Back then, I was in love with you...and I was happy and content and I couldn't help it."

So Miu's story wasn't a lie.

And that transparent world filled with kindness, those gentle feelings, the exuberant light—everything written in that book was the truth for me back then.

"Miu...would you...see me now? I wonder if we could ever see each other again..."

Ever since the accident, I'd wanted to see Miu with all my heart.

The terrestrial stars scattered on the tree glittered quietly.

My heart swelled, my throat prickled, I grew desolate and morose, I felt totally alone, and I crouched down on the grass and was on the verge of tears when a gentle voice called my name.

"Konoha."

When I turned around, Tohko was standing there with a placid smile on her face, wearing a long coat.

I frantically rubbed at my eyes with the back of my hand.

"Where did you come from all of a sudden?"

"Somehow, I thought you might come here...Here's your present."

She gently deposited one of the ribboned bags that she had been handing out at the party into my hand.

Inside were some star-shaped candy and a stuffed bear wearing a Santa suit.

"Did you come here just to give me this? To this abandoned place? It's dangerous for a girl by herself."

"It's fine. You'll be with me when I go back, after all," she evaded flippantly, not listening to a word of my scolding. Then Tohko tilted her head and peeked up into my face. "So where's my present?"

"There isn't one."

I hurriedly turned my face away, thinking she'd caught me looking teary.

"Geez."

She pouted for a moment, then chuckled maturely.

"Don't be like that. Gimme something. *It doesn't have to be something big.*"

At those words I recalled the bookmark that I'd stuck in my student planner. When I pulled it out of the planner and held it out to her, Tohko put out both hands to accept it.

When she saw my cell phone number and my e-mail address written on it, her eyes crinkled.

"Sincerely—it's like a letter. Or like...from the heart or genuinely or truly...like that..."

The words of my e-mail address were borrowed from a song that I liked.

Tohko softly pressed the bookmark to her lips.

In the light of the moon and the glittering of the Christmas tree, my heart skipped a beat at that gesture, which seemed so like a ritual.

"It's so *sweet*...like candied violets."

Her petal-like lips beamed delicately.

Then she popped the bookmark into her mouth and began making quiet crunching noises as she chewed.

She swallowed the very last scrap and—

With a smile, she said, "Ahhh, that was delicious. Thank you."

I stared at her blankly.

"Oh—what's wrong? Konoha?"

"You ate it."

"Huh?"

"You ate my cell phone number and e-mail address."

"Whaaaat? I wasn't supposed to eat it?"

"An e-mail address isn't a meal or even a snack!"

"What? What? What's an e-mail address?"

Apparently Tohko the Luddite had never realized what it was.

"Forget it."

I spun around to turn my back on her, crouched down on the grass, and hugged my knees.

Uh-oh. When I let my guard down, the tears came welling back up.

"…Um…er, can I…sit next to you?"

"You can, but don't look at me."

My vision was growing slowly indistinct, and a hot lump rose in my throat.

Tohko sat down on the grass with her back against mine. Below her coat she was still evidently wearing her Santa costume, and she pulled the hem down against a chill and hugged her knees.

As soon as my concern about her seeing my tears went away, the tears pooling in the corners of my eyes dropped down my cheeks. I wondered why I got so teary whenever Tohko was with me.

"Were you thinking about Omi?"

"About lots of stuff."

"The party was fun, wasn't it? It was a nice break."

"You take too many breaks, Tohko."

"It's fine. I'm gonna knock out a whole math workbook when I get home."

"It's not a first-year workbook, is it?"

"How rude. It's a second-year book."

"You don't think this is totally hopeless?"

"I'm planning to get to the third-year problems before the test!"

As my voice hitched and I bit back sobs, Tohko went on with her ordinary conversation.

I was pretty sure she had already discovered I'd been crying, but…

While she gazed up at the sky, Tohko had taken hold of my right hand without my noticing.

Her warm, gentle grip—

"No snow fell, but look how pretty the moon is, Konoha. There's a sentence about this in Chekhov's 'In the Ravine.'"

In the pale moonlight, her clear voice flowed like a hymn that purified the soul.

"'However great the evil, still the night is calm and beautiful and, still there is and will be in this world a truth as calm and beautiful. And everything on earth is eagerly awaiting its union with that truth, as the moonlight unites with the night'...Ahhh, now I want to eat some Chekhov," Tohko said rapturously.

The truth wasn't necessarily totally beautiful.

There existed ugly and painful truths that made you want to look away from them.

But the night enveloped everything, and the moon shone down on us unchanging.

There were things that didn't change and beautiful things.

The gentleness, the warmth of Tohko's hand had taught me that.

I knew the reason I didn't become a Phantom is because I met Tohko.

Because she held my hand like this.

Because she said important things to me.

I hoped that somewhere on his long journey, the other version of me who had decided to never sing again and had gone away would meet a person with a kind touch.

Please, please, God.

As I prayed, Tohko murmured kindly to me, "Konoha...even if I'm not around anymore, don't stop writing okay?"

And without understanding why Tohko would say something

like that right now, my heart squeezed tighter than I could stand at the sadness and intensity in her voice.

Are you saying I have to send you snacks even after you graduate? I wanted to snipe back, but the words stuck in my throat.

"Do you think Miu Inoue will write another book?"

A question I'd been unable to answer.

But if Miu Inoue were to write another book—if he were to read it under some other sky—it was unlikely, but—

If that happened, maybe he would sing again, too.

In the spring, Tohko would be gone.

I couldn't keep sniffling and crying forever. I had to become strong.

But for now, I was happy to feel the warmth of Tohko's hand; I was relieved, and while I let my tears spill quietly out, I continued my prayers to the moon.

On the holy night the child of God came down to earth, I prayed for the happiness of Omi, of Kotobuki, and of Miu.

———◆———

Nanase sent Yuka a Christmas card over e-mail.

There was a message that said she would always be best friends with Yuka; then she said that she'd replied to the e-mail from Inoue's old girlfriend.

Saying that no matter how badly she talked about Inoue, no matter how mean she was, she wouldn't lose faith.

That she would only believe what Inoue told her.

That tomorrow she was going to see Miu Asakura—

Hello, Mizuki Nomura here! The fourth story in the *Book Girl* series has arrived!

I'm *SO* sorry to everyone who expected Miu to show up!! I'm definitely not just messing with you. I always planned for Kotobuki to star in this one.

After all, if we went straight into the Miu story with Konoha still playing everything off, I would just feel so sorry for Kotobuki... This time, Konoha's classmate finally took a step forward.

And so, the fourth story is *The Phantom of the Opera*. The Phantom is just so heartrending. I'm always moved, no matter how often I read it. There are a lot of interpretations of the Phantom in plays, movies, and novels, so it's really interesting to compare them all! They each have their own flavor.

Speaking of flavor... the sugar tart that Tohko talks about in the opening scene is a dessert that I'm personally attached to. I only tasted it once more than ten years ago, but when I went looking for it again, I got an intense craving for it. It appears that using vergeoise made from sugar beets is the most common way of making it. And it looks really good, too!

When I'm writing Tohko's meal scenes, I remember a flavor

and think back on it, so I get hungry. It's kind of a problem. But actually, in all the books up until now, I've only mixed in *one* thing that I absolutely hate and would never eat!

On to the thank-yous: Yuka wanting to live inside a Christmas tree is taken from the words of the performer Ms. Atsuko Enomoto, whom I heard as a guest on the radio. It was right at the time I was creating the plot for the fourth story, so I *begged* her to let me use it, and she did.

Ms. Enomoto, thank you for your gracious consideration.

Also Ms. Miho Takeoka, thank you sooooo much for your great pictures this time around!

I'm always running right up to the page limit, and it's always hectic—I'm sorry!—but in the next volume it will, at last, be a story about "her" and Konoha, so please read it! See you then!

Mizuki Nomura
April 1, 2007

AFTERWORD

Those were the illustrations
for the 4th volume, the
painful-but-fun Nana
Se Installment (?).

As always and ever, my
editor was an astounding
help. I'm gonna be a
better girl next time...

Miho Takeda

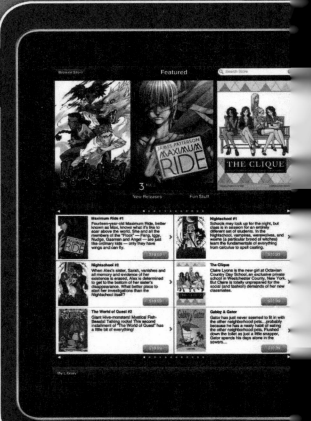